THE BOOKSTORE SERIES

PASSAGE OF TIME

Part 1

I0628566

ALICE VL

THE BOOKSTORE SERIES
Passage of Time – Book 1

Alice VL

THE BOOKSTORE SERIES
Passage of Time – Book 1

Copyright 2018

Alice VL's The Bookstore Series

BOOK 1

PASSAGE OF TIME

Alice VL

THE BOOKSTORE SERIES

Passage of Time – Book 1

Alice VL

THE BOOKSTORE SERIES
Passage of Time – Book 1

TABLE OF CONTENTS

THE BOOKSTORE SERIES
Passage of Time – Book 1

Alice VL

INTRODUCTION

She cast down her eyes and bowed her head just as her legs became shaky underneath her. Sarah was convinced that the ground beneath her feet were cruelly giving way below her before she fell to her knees and collapsed onto the ground.

She was thoroughly vanquished by the grief that had begun as subtle waves, before it created a continuous ripple and began drowning her. She was wholly defeated and effectively beleaguered by the unanticipated devastation she had come home to, only a few short hours ago.

She unabashedly allowed her tears to gush from her eyes before she wrapped her arms around her stomach, and made no apology for falling apart in such a public place. She was overwhelmed and frazzled by the severe pain she was exposed to, a torment that struck into the inner core of her soul.

As she gasped for the breaths that were beginning to evade her, she was sure that her heart was being mercilessly ripped out from inside of her, and when the pain turned physical, she was certain that her lungs were being ruthlessly crushed by two strong, invisible and malicious hands.

Her breathing had become an automated fight for survival, as she clung to each breath she managed to inhale, when her entire body began to shudder violently. "Danny!"

She shouted out through the last of the gasping breaths she was only just able to muster up. The tears had begun to inexorably flood her face, and when she looked up one more time, she knew that what she had seen written in stone only a moment ago, was something she had never expected to see. It was something she could never have anticipated coming home to someday.

The name that was so coldly written in stone was a name she could in no way at all, accept as his name and ultimately, his destiny. It could not have been what fate had in store for her; it could not be so cruel and heartless. As she waged an inner battle with her heart and her soul, she closed her eyes and cursed the universe for plunging her into a limitless well that was spilling over with severe misery and acute agony.

She was flung into a kind of despair, she had never

known before, one she could not predict or see coming as she reflected on her childhood. The affirmation that was staring back at her, of what she could hardly abide to be true, was imprinted in a boulder right in front of the eyes. A confirmation that had not quite yet reached her soul, but that was callously blinding her eyes by the tempest that had begun surging inside of them. As she desperately scrutinized the gravestone in absolute incredulity and downright horror, she damned to hell all that was revealed to her only a few short breaths ago. She condemned the haunting words that were engraved on that tomb stone into a kind of hell she had only just been introduced to, and unwillingly became acquainted with, one that had heartlessly paralyzed and wholly shattered her heart into a million fragmented shards.

It was a kind of anguish she had never known before, or could barely imagine she could feel, and walk away from, leaving her heart intact. It had pitilessly spilled over from her heart, and into the very center of the innermost core of her. It had crept up on her like a dormant parasite, and physically debilitated her when she least expected it. It consumed her from the inside out, until she could no longer identify or distinguish between any part of her body that had escaped the severe, brutal and immobilizing torture.

Alice VL

She rubbed ferociously at the tears that were continuously blinding her, as she frantically tried to unclutter her face that had begun to disappear and hide behind her wild and unruly hair. She took in a deep breath, desperate to swallow back on a callous, yet narrowing lump in her throat, as she slowly read the words that were to be eternally engraved on the tomb stone in front of her. She read it out softly and repeatedly, as she frantically pleaded with her eyes to deceive her, if only just once. Just once, she wanted to let out a sigh of relief that what she had seen was all one enormous mistake, and breathe once again, without restraint. Just once, she wanted to close her eyes as she shut off the murky puddles of salty tears that were spilling from her eyes, and onto her face. Just once, she wanted to laugh out loud, and lightheartedly criticize her eyes for misleading her. But, each time she read his name out loud, she was harshly reminded of his leaving. The date was there, right in front of her, and it was viciously taunting her.

The permanent imprints before her, verified the fact that Daniel Kingsley had left their world, and exchanged it for another, only a few short months ago. Two dates were imprinted on that very stone, one to indicate a beginning of a man she would love for the remainder of her life, and another to bring her to her knees, and rip a part of her away with him.

Alice VL

THE BOOKSTORE SERIES
Passage of Time – Book 1

She was not prepared to walk into Hazel Creek's only cemetery and find him lying in the ground beneath her. Her heart was not yet ready to understand, and it was in no way at all, equipped to let him go. It was an end date that showed to her, a moment in time that simply stopped a once beating heart. A heart she had clung to and yearned for, for almost all her life. A heart she was so sure, would continue to beat for her, as it waited for her to come home.

A date that signified a day where his world had ended, and her love simply ceased to exist, almost as though he never was. A heart that did not need her permission to die, and certainly did not ask for her approval.

His heart, Daniel's heart had died, and left hers behind, battered and bruised, and to carry on beating without him. If not for the date impressed on the exact same stone that reminded her that his heart had in fact, begun beating for the very first time almost a lifetime ago, she could swear that that same stone was horrifically taunting her, and cruelly cleaving at the splintered pieces of her already shattered heart.

'Daniel Kingsley 18/5/1966 – 21/3/2000'

She was too late. Sarah Swanson had returned home

Alice VL

almost eleven months too late. She was a lifetime apart and a universe removed from the only man that once made sense to her own thumping heart. She laid her head down on his grave and pulled her knees up to her chin, before she gently rocked herself back and forth. She cried out in anguish when the pain became almost too much to endure. "Danny, don't leave me here without you …"

She closed her eyes and could clearly see the haunting vision of his eyes, looking back at her. She had safely kept the image of him burnt in her mind and scorched in her heart from the moment she had left him behind.

She folded her arms around her legs and sobbed fiercely as she laid down on the final resting place of the man she had loved for entire life. The man she had promised to return to once she had found her own worth. Once she had found a reason to justify his love for her, a validation she so desperately sought. She had made a decision to someday, come home to him, deserving of his love.

The man she had pleaded with to wait for her, while she built a diamond-studded ladder to the stars, and stepped on everyone. The man she had adored with every single beat of her now aching heart.

Alice VL

THE BOOKSTORE SERIES
Passage of Time – Book 1

The man that she thought was larger than her, larger than any functioning human being, larger than life. The man she was so sure would never leave her. The man she never once considered, could die.

"Give him back to me …" She pleaded desperately, as she lay sobbing on the ground that had coldly separated her from him.

Alice VL

THE BOOKSTORE SERIES
Passage of Time – Book 1

Alice VL

THE BOOKSTORE SERIES
Passage of Time – Book 1

DEDICATION

The world still turns. The seasons still come and the seasons still go. Autumn changes the color of the leaves and with winter comes the cold and the snow. In spring, the world cheers at the sight of blossoming flowers and new beginnings. And then, in summer, laughter fills and lingers in the air. The world still turns.

The streets are filled with the sounds of cars making their way down the roads, and the voices of people on city pavements still echo in the distance. Children are still born each day. Lovers fall in love and lovers fall out of love, every single day. Death comes for those whose time is up, but the world still turns. Mornings still come with each new sunrise, and the darkness covers the universe with each sunset.

The world awakes, the world goes to sleep, and the world still turns. But hers doesn't. Her world stood still a long time ago.

Alice VL

It no longer turns. It has kept her trapped in a kind of a limbo she can't get out of; one she just can't escape from. Everything around her changes, yet nothing is different. Her world stood still. Her life has been rocked and her heart is shattered. But, for the rest there is not even a slight indication from the universe that something has changed; something so important to someone so much lesser has been lost.

There is nothing to tell her that his leaving has somehow impacted the world, shoved it off-course or shook it slightly off its track. Like it did her. Like it shoved her to the ground, and kept her there. There is nothing to tell her that he was important to this world, to this life, and to her heart. Yet, while the world forgets him, she searches for him at the break of each day, and at the last light of each night. She looks for him between the walls of the home he once lived in. She traces the footprints of a life he once existed so profoundly in.

She follows the trails he once took on the city streets, and she continues all the way down to the dirt roads he once found solace in. She retraces the paths he took to the beach, and she follows his tracks to the forest. She looks for him. She keeps looking for him. She still looks for him. She tries to find him in crowds. She hunts for proof that he was once real. She clings to photographs, and she holds onto the memory of him. She doesn't want the world to forget. *She* doesn't want to forget. And still, the world turns without him. She so wishes it didn't.

THE BOOKSTORE SERIES
Passage of Time – Book 1

Alice VL

PART ONE

Sarah Swanson came home on that cold day in February, eleven months too late. She couldn't quite decipher how many sunrises she had missed in Hazel Creek, or how many sunsets there were since she had been gone. She returned home on that ghostly, overcast day, just as she once professed she would.

What turned out to be almost an entire existence ago, far removed from the days when she was still a bright-eyed teenager with a million dreams and a gazillion smiles in her heart, she swore diligently that she would come back to him, and back to her home in Hazel Creek.

She came home to the village she had left her soul behind in, just like she said she would come back to reclaim someday. Just as soon as she had found her wonderful, and just as soon as she had reached the stars she had aimed for, after her many conversations and negotiations with the moon, when she was just a little girl. She found her way home and back to the village that had kept her heart securely tucked away in its palms since

Alice VL

she had left almost a thousand moons ago, and as it turned out, a promise too late.

She came home to the village that had unwearyingly sat on the sidelines and watched her dream, while carefully guiding her on all the roads she had walked on as a child. The same village that had ultimately led her to the crossroads she would come to, and the road she would end up choosing someday.

She had to run as fast as her legs could carry her as she tried to follow the storms that were raging underneath her feet. She came home to the little town that had kept her safe and shielded from the rest of the world for most of her life, before it had finally raised her. She came home on that gloomy, wretched day to the houses she once knew so well, and the trees she had found shade in on so many scorching days.

She bowed before the school she had found family in, to the people she had adored, and the children who had now all grown up. She came home on that cold and rainy day, to faces that had changed, and names that were no longer the same. She came home to a religion her little hometown had passed on to her, from the very moment she was born.

She was too young to understand, and not old enough to

know that it would someday be the home, she would leave and when it was someday too late, she would return and leave all that she thought had mattered to her, behind.

A town she would run back to as she left the bright city lights behind her. A home she would return to, where the streets knew her trail and the skies recognized her shadow, only, it would be one promise too late.

She came home to the mountains that echoed the childlike laughter that once used to hang in the air as they climbed to the top, where they would sit together and watch the sun set over their little home town. It was almost as though a curtain to a stage was being drawn, and they, the audience.

She came home to the waves that continued to whisper their names as they crashed heartlessly onto the shore, as though to remind her that her soul had remained behind, yet, it continued to linger somewhere in between the stars and the oceans of Hazel Creek.

She came home to the paved streets and farm roads that would continue to lead her to the one place her heart had found a home in all those moons ago. She came home to the leafy branches of trees that once blew endless messages of love into her ears, as she walked through the dirt roads, and whispered to the clouds.

It was not that long ago that she had left her village, and her love behind. It was not that long ago that she swore to him she would return, just as soon as she had found and captured her radiance. She said that she would bring all her wonderful with her and she promised to share it with him someday. She vowed that she would never forget him, or the village that her roots were firmly planted in.

She asked him to wait for her, and she begged him to believe in her. She nervously whispered in his ear that she was sure the city streets might be paved in emerald stones, and that the morning sun might shine a little brighter over there.

She told him that she was afraid that the city lights and urban stars at night might perhaps blind her as she sets out in search of her magnificence. She told him that she thought the nights might be shorter, and that her days could perhaps, be a little warmer. She was sure that she could get lost in the crowds of a thousand strangers on the city streets, as she quietly and inconspicuously, searched for her glory.

She thought that she could become fabulous and be

incredible before she came home again to the village that she knew, was keeping her heritage nourished and watered. She thought that she could grow up and earn her merit in the world, before she came home to win him, and conquer him forever.

But, as she lay rocking back and forth on the cold grave beneath her, she wondered how she never knew that her value was by no means at all, found in her search for wonderful. She continuously chastised herself as she questioned her motives over and over again.

But, how she was to know that her splendor would not mean much at all, and that her hunt would ultimately be all for nothing, without him? As she lay cradling her legs, she realized that her coming home had turned out to be a promise too late.

How was she to know that her glory was inside of her, all along? How could she ever have known that when she finally came home, she would come home to a worthlessness she never thought she would feel in the town that once filled her with butterflies and bubbles?

She came home today, just like she once swore she would, yet, nothing was as it once was. "I came home today, Danny …" She whispered through the tears that continued to cruelly bucket from her eyes, as though she had an endless supply.

She had found her much desired wonderful and she became extraordinary for him, only it was not the kind she went in search of. It was in him. It was in her. It lay quiescent in them, in their love and in their togetherness. It was there, in their eyes and in their laughter. It was there, right in the midst of their childhood, and it followed them into their adulthood. She once thought that she had caught a glimpse of it, when they shared their very first kiss. She could have sworn that she once felt it in his touch and saw it in his eyes. "I came home today ..."

She swallowed back on an imprisoning knot in her throat and understood for the very first time that it was right there inside of her and inside of him, from the moment he had walked into her life. Without him, none of what she had set out to attain mattered anymore, and not much made sense to her. For all the books she had written, and all the adventures she had been on, none of it could compare to the value his love had found in her.

All her achievements and each of her so-called accomplishments seemed utterly inconsequential and highly insignificant, without him. She had left to find her extraordinary for him, and now he would never know.

Alice VL

She had found all she had ever searched for, and all she thought she would ever need, yet it was nothing like where she thought she would find her joy and importance in. She was wrong. She had searched for all the wrong things, in all the wrong places. It was in him. It had always been in him, and his unyielding love for her.

To come home, and miss out on the years that were, were never in any of her plans or her dreams. Yet, she constantly had one more step to take, and one more road to follow before she could return to Hazel Creek, and home to him. Year after year, she told him that she had one more conquest, and one more dream to pursue, and that she swore, she would be home soon.

She was never quite able to touch the stars she was so frantic to grab a hold of, and she stopped whispering to the moon nearly a thousand nights before. It was as though she could almost reach them, and with each attempt, and every effort she made, she was certain that they were only moments away from her grasp.

She never thought that he would leave. It did not once cross her mind that he would give up on her, or that he would relinquish his fight, and surrender to a darkness she could in no way at all, ever find him in. She never thought that his trail would be covered and disguised by the sands of time.

She never once imagined that all she would be left with someday would be his name written in stone, on an abandoned and forlorn spot in Hazel Creek, one she never thought she'd find him in. She never thought that her village would grow up just as they did and change just as they had.

She never thought that the faces she once knew so well would be gone from the only home they had ever known. She never thought that she would be welcomed by a whole lot of emptiness, and that nothing would be the same when she finally found her way home again.

She never thought that their little hometown would appear as a total stranger to her, with odd new people and unfamiliar, new buildings. She never thought that the trees that were once a part of their creed, would be cold-heartedly cut down, and that their mountain would be covered by brand-new houses.

She never thought that he would leave. She never thought that he could leave. She never once thought she would dwell in a world without him. She never once imagined that she would be compelled to exist in a world, he was no longer a part of. She never thought that she would be a promise too late.

Alice VL

PART TWO

When Sarah drove into Hazel Creek and through the streets of the village that was still holding possessively onto her heart and her ancestry, for the very first time in almost fifteen years, she understood for how she had recklessly and mistakenly convinced herself that it was essential to leave and go in search of her very own kind of remarkable.

How foolish she had been, and how utterly deluded her young and untaught mind was. She was already extraordinary for him. She never needed to pursue any kind of fabulous, he had already spotted that in her. Just like him, she had come from a village with its very own fairytales and enchantments, and that was all the wonderful they had ever needed.

She came home today, to discover that he had found his own kind of exquisite, his very own fairytale, and his very precious wonderful. He had been whispering to his angel at night about new sunrises and brand-new sunsets. They had spoken of a place where he could see the sun rise again, and where the streets were paved in gold, and lined with flowery blossoms.

He had found his delight in the echoing of the moon, in the whispers of the stars, and in the drops of the rain. He had spoken to his angel about finding a place where his soul could rest for a while, and where his heart could love her without distance, and without hurting as much as it had until then.

He asked about taking one final breath over here, and he whispered about taking another first one, over there. There, where his eyes could once again see through the foggy mists that were blinding him over here. There, where his heart could be unbroken, and where he was no longer breathing simply for her return.

He asked his angel to close his eyes, but not to let hers cry. He said that she could never know, and he begged that she would never return, and discover the horrifying secret he had kept hidden from her. He told his angel that he knew how she always felt she had to run, but that he just never really understood why.

He said that sometimes in the darkest moments of the night, and from the very moment she had left, he could sometimes feel her fall entirely apart under their stormy skies, but that he was sure, she still wouldn't come home any time soon.

He told his angel that he could feel somewhere deep inside of him, that there had to be a little more out there for him, and that he could at times and in certain moments, feel the rumbling rampant underneath his own feet, as they nudged him to find his own kind of wonderful.

He told his angel that he was exhausted and weary, and that he could no longer wrestle with the demons of the disease that had thoroughly invaded and pitilessly ravaged his entire body, before it ruthlessly attacked his mind.

He said that he'd hate for her to see him broken and defeated by the one battle he could not conquer, and that they both knew it would be one combat he would eventually surrender to. He asked his angel, if it could perhaps be his turn to find his very own forever, away from their village and away from their world.

With the Kingsleys and the Swansons all gathered around his bedside, Daniel sluggishly glanced over at them, one by one. He smiled bravely at the familiar and loving faces that gazed crushingly back at him. With each eye he met, a tear rolled for him and the courageous battle he had fought for so long.

One by one, they took his hand, and when Anabel begged him to fight for just a while longer, Daniel slowly placed his finger on his lips, and weakly squeezed her hand, "Don't tell Sarah."

Cindy wiped the tears from her eyes, and walked up to him, before she placed her hand on his shoulder, "Danny?" Daniel turned to face her, and smiled wretchedly, "Don't tell Sarah. You must protect her from this. Don't break her heart. She will, she'll never forgive herself. Let her have her bright city lights, and golden pavements ..." Daniel's voice trailed off, as he fought to keep his eyes open. "I love her, I love you, all of you. I am so sorry." He whispered breathlessly before he closed his eyes one last time.

On a cold, dark winter's night, his angel answered him for the very first time. He stood at his bedside and wiped the warm tears that were escaping from the corners of his eyes. He placed his hand on his cheek, and took pity on Daniel's prolonged suffering. "Alright ..." He whispered as he gently stroked his hair. He assured Daniel that Sarah would not return soon, but that a field filled with roses and angels were ready to take his hand, and guide him home.

Alice VL

THE BOOKSTORE SERIES
Passage of Time – Book 1

They were ready to walk with him to where his fairytale and ever-after awaited him. They were ready to show him a place they had prepared for him, there where he would be free from the body that was savagely ravaged by an illness they discovered too late. On that chilly, shadowy winter's night, his angel closed his eyes, and led Daniel away, and to his forever.

At that very moment, and almost a thousand miles away, on the corner of a busy and bustling city street, Sarah caught a glimpse of an artist behind his easel as people hurriedly passed him by, almost as though he was fiercely guarded from the world around him. He smiled bashfully as he clutched a paint brush in his hand, and whistled a love song that could not be drowned out by the lively noises of the streets.

With each brush stroke, he brought to life the waves of an ocean that were crashing harshly on the sands of a beach. She stood silently as she watched him paint the seas that reflected the rising sun of the morning sky.

She gazed longingly at the life he was creating by the mere strokes of his brush, and through the gentle whistles of his love songs. With each motion, she was reminded of the village she had left behind, and the beauty of the love she was sure, had forgotten her.

Alice VL

With a trouncing heart, she walked up to him and through the shudders of her own voice, she asked him if he only painted scenes of the oceans and the skies? He lowered his brush and grinned, before he told her that for a few bucks, he would paint her anything she wanted.

She fell to her knees and grabbed his warm, aesthetic hands. She stared at them, confident and hopeful that they would create a painting for her too. She asked him if he could paint her a love story. Without pausing to take a breath, she went on to describe how it should look, and that it had to be just as she had planned when she was only a little girl.

She told him of a little blue house, a slight way out of town. She asked him to paint a porch with a swing, so that she could watch over her horses and gaze out onto her flower fields. She begged him to paint her on that swing in a white cotton dress and make it the very first day of spring. She squeezed his hands tighter, and asked him again, to paint her a love story.

His heart began to batter wildly when he noticed the despair in her persuasive eyes. He hurriedly seized a blank canvas, and picked up his paint brush. He asked her where she would like him to place her love in the painting, and when she began to whimper softly, he knew he would have to be placed

Alice VL

right beside her, where she needed him to be.

She asked him if he could perhaps peek into her heart and see how it longed for the way it was before. Before, when her story was a painting she had once owned. And then, she implored him to place her love's arms back around her, just like it once was.

She told him how the bright sunrises contradicted the dense mist that weighed down so heavily on her. She said that she needed him to paint the joyful sounds of the birds in the mornings, so that her heart could hear them once more. She gently whispered how she wondered why the world continued to turn, and that without her new painting, she was just not sure she could begin again.

She asked him to add fireflies to brighten her darkest nights, and she told him to place the stars like a silvery gown around her. She said that she wanted to hang it above her big, empty bed where she feared the dark and dreaded the dawn, all at the same time. She softly confessed, that she reaches for her love in vain, and that she tearfully whispers his name, just as she is about to fall asleep.

She reminded the artist not to forget to paint daffodils, so that she can smile instead of cry. She told him to take his time because at that very moment, her heart does not yet have a home, and that it was just a painting, until it becomes her love story.

Through her tears, she told him that she had left him behind, and that she no longer knew how to find her way home. She said that she had been gone for so long, much longer than she had planned. She whispered how he told her to forget him, just as he had forgotten her. "My heart can't let go ..."

She dabbed at the tears that were shimmering in her eyes, before they rolled onto her cheeks. As he painted her love story, she noticed how he was painting the image of the man back home that she had lost, even though her heart would not allow her to find another. She gasped for air when she saw him come alive in the painting, and when the artist caught her just as her legs caved in beneath her, she whispered sadly, "How did you know?"

He sat her down on his little chair in front of the easel. When she gazed over at the man her heart was aching for as he stared back at her, the man trapped in her canvassed love story, she slowly traced his entire face with her fingertips.

He was older than she remembered, but his eyes were as frosty as they had been when she looked into them for the very first time, an entire lifetime ago. The lines around his eyes told her of how often he had laughed while she was gone, and the frown lines on his forehead swore to her that he thought of her often.

The sadness she found in the grooves around his mouth told her that he might have missed her once in a while, just as she had longed for him each night while she was gone. The silver streaks that were beginning to invade the peppery hair told her that he had spent too many nights alone, and that she had fallen asleep too many nights without him.

It was the man she had left behind, even though he had grown older and seemed as though he was conquered by sorrow. As her tears began rolling desolately from her eyes, she thanked the artist and took her painting.

THE BOOKSTORE SERIES
Passage of Time – Book 1

Alice VL

PART THREE

When she drove into her hometown for the first time since she had left Hazel Creek, Sarah Swanson reached for her phone and excitedly dialed Simone Watts' number, anxious to get in touch with her, and see her again after all the years.

She was frantic to shrug off her fears, and she was sure that Simone could better prepare her for her return. As she gazed around her, she could almost feel him again, but she could hardly discard the terror that had begun to overwhelm her, by the mere thought of seeing Daniel again.

She felt a shudder run through her entire body and was at once thankful that Simone had taken her call without delay. "Simmy, it's me ..."

"Who?"

"Me, Sarah ..."

"Sè! How are you?"

"Are you at work?"

"Yep. All day, every day." "I'll see you in a bit?"

"You're here? In Hazel Creek?"

"Yeah …"

"Wow! Okay … just look for Super Sim Styles, on the corner of 2nd and Harley. Okay?"

"Thanks, Simmy, see you in a bit!"

Sarah had met Simone midway through grade two when Simone had moved to Hazel Creek from the city when she was barely eight years old. Sarah took pity on her when she found her having her sandwiches alone during their lunch hour. She felt badly for the new girl, who had not yet made friends, and at once invited her to sit with her. "Hello. My name is Sarah."

"Hey, I'm Simone …"

"Where are you from?"

"Canterbury."

"Oh? The City! Have you made any friends here yet?"

"No …"

"So, I'll be your friend if you like. You can sit with me and we can sit together in class, if you like?"

Simone smiled broadly when Sarah extended a hand to her, and walked her over to her lunch table. She hurriedly introduced Simone to the rest of her group, and quickly opened a seat for her to take right beside her.

They were an odd pair when they became inseparable in the years that followed. To most of the world, their friendship seemed an unlikely alliance.

Simone Watts was the only child of Charles and Maggie Watts, both teachers at Hazel Creek's only high school. Simone was almost a full head shorter than Sarah, even though she was a couple of months older.

Sarah often chuckled softly when she scrutinized Simone, and regularly teased her when she once told her that she must be the secret love child of a Greek god. She bore no resemblance to her parents, and Sarah often wondered whether Simone's appearance had perhaps been inherited from her grandparents. "You must look like your grandmother?" Sarah joked as they sat in the library, one afternoon after school.

"No ..."

Simone giggled when she noticed the frustration on Sarah's face. She was enormously proud of her long, raven black hair, with eyes that seemed darker than at the very dead of night. "Well then, you're adopted! You must be!"

Simone burst out laughing, before she finally put Sarah out of her misery, "My grandfather is from Spain. I look like his mother, my great grandmother …"

Simone was petite and timid, but what she lacked in height, she made up for in her playful personality, and infectious laughter. She was beautiful and kind, but almost as though a switch had been flicked, she would become quiet and utterly withdrawn at times.

Sarah discovered very early on that Simone was shy, and that being an only child, had kept her caged and guarded from the rest of the world. Her parents, both teachers, had kept her on her toes, and Sarah couldn't help but pity her from time to time.

Charles and Maggie Watts were strict parents, but it was nothing more than their love for Simone that had kept them protective over their only daughter. Even though Simone was permitted afternoons out at the bookstore with Sarah, they very rarely agreed to sleepovers or outings away from Hazel Creek.

Sarah, on the other hand, was only too happy to flaunt her long blonde hair that trailed down her back and past her waist. She was pale, but her hazel green eyes were striking and large, and it would often appear as though there were murky puddles that would spill out into her eyes, during a stormy and tempestuous night.

She was popular at school, and she adored the attention her teachers, brothers and sisters would bestow upon her. She would often remind her sisters that as the youngest of five children, she was and would remain the apple of her parents' eye.

Sarah would converse freely, and without filtering her words. She would often be the victim of her extroverted personality that persistently landed her in more trouble than she cared to admit to.

She was the youngest daughter of Thomas and Cindy Swanson, who would regularly introduce her as their untamed child. They would apologize in advance for the daughter who would speak her mind and fight for her place in their family, and in the world.

Alice VL

Thomas and Cindy knew that Sarah came into this world without any brakes, and that she would rarely apologize for saying what she felt without consideration the implications thereof, even though it was inappropriate most of the time.

Even though they had little to no desire to restrain or tame her, they hoped that she would sieve through her words more carefully as she grew older. Sarah treasured her parents and knew from the deepest and most central part of her that she was tiring, and a handful at the best of times.

Without apologizing for her uncultivated words, Sarah would often place her arms around her parents as a way of expressing regret for her persuasiveness, and subsequent lack of tact.

It was as though it had become an unwritten agreement that her remorse would be found in a loving embrace that she would have ready for her parents and her siblings, especially after one of her tempestuous outbursts.

As much as she adored her parents, Sarah was wholly besotted with her sisters Megan and Claire, while she secretly worshipped her brothers Benjamin and Robert. She would watch from the sidelines as Megan fell in love often, and she would secretly stand on the other side of her bedroom door, and hear her weep into her pillow with each broken heart she would endure as a result. Megan loved fiercely, and she loved unequivocally.

Cindy often told Thomas how she thought that Megan was simply in love with the idea of love, and that she was not sure how much more bruising or battering her heart could endure.

Sarah loathed the fact that Megan's heart was shattered so often, and she swore that hers would remain intact, and that she would someday, choose someone who would love her so much more than she could ever be capable of loving him.

Megan was barely two years older than Sarah, but she dreamed of having a house filled with children someday. She was desperate to become a mother, and desired having children more than anything else in the world.

After she had graduated from high school, she enrolled in college without delay, and completed her very first teaching diploma a short three years later. Even though she had met David Dawson in high school, she married him a month after she graduated from college.

They had settled into a suburban home in Hazel Creek

where Megan took up a teaching position at Hazel Creek Primary School. Within three years, Sarah became the proud aunt of a niece, Melissa, and a nephew, Michael, even though she had never met them.

She had left for Queenstown a few months after her eighteenth birthday, almost a year before Megan and David were married. Megan and Cindy were equally devastated when Sarah failed to return for the wedding or show up for the birth of either of her children.

"Honey, it's your sister's wedding?" Cindy had made a desperate attempt to convince Sarah to return to Hazel Creek for Megan's wedding a week before she was due to get married. "We haven't seen you in a year, and she so much wants you to be a bridesmaid."

"I know, mommy, and I'm sorry. I just can't. I'll be out of town for a month, possibly more. I can't back out, I am under contract …"

Sarah was frantic to explain her commitments and justify her absence, even though she felt immense guilt for failing to make a bigger effort.

"I don't understand, Sarah. We can't come visit you, you

won't let Daniel come and see you, what's going on?"

"Nothing's going on, mom. I am never here. I am always on the road or in the air. I can't cancel my bookings. I can't do that, not now while I am still trying to establish myself. This is a tough industry to break into, you know that, mom?"

Cindy sighed and gently shook her head. "It's been a year, Sarah. You said just a year. You said you wanted to go to the city for just one year."

"I know that. I just cannot dictate my schedule to my agent or publishers. I just need a little more time here. I am so close to achieving all the things I came here to do. If I give up now, it would all have been for nothing."

"Sarah, you are missing out on the things that are important. You are going to look back someday and regret the time you spent chasing the wrong things. It could all be gone in the blink of an eye."

"Oh mother, I'll be home soon, you'll see. Tell Megs I love her, and I hope her day is as beautiful as she is. Please send me photographs of the wedding?"

Cindy remained silent when she realized that Sarah was

bewitched by the glamour she had found in the city, and that she would not be home anytime soon. "I love you, mom."

"I love you too, Sè …"

Sarah ended her call to her mother and hurriedly dialed Daniel's number. "Sè?"

"Hey Danny …" She was at once eerily silenced when she heard his familiar, comforting voice.

"You are coming up for Meg's wedding, right?"

"I can't, Danny. I am flying out to St. Rose's on Thursday."

"Come on, Sarah! It's your sister's wedding! The first wedding in your family!"

"I know, Danny, there's nothing I can do. I just can't take time off now. I have commitments and obligations that I can't just cancel. But Danny, I wanted to ask you, I mean, I haven't seen you in a year, and, do you want to join me in St. Rose's for the weekend?"

Daniel remained silent for what felt like an eternity. "I can't Sarah, I can't skip Megan's wedding. And you shouldn't either."

Alice VL

"You're right. So, I'll speak to you soon?"

"Whatever, Sarah. When are you coming home, for good?"

"I don't know, Danny, I just have so much still to do, maybe next year?"

Daniel closed his eyes, before he ran his fingers through his hair, "Right …"

"I'll come visit soon, I promise …"

"Yeah, tell Megan that. Anyway, I have to run, take care!"

Before she could respond, Daniel had abruptly ended their phone call. Sarah sat down on the edge of her bed, and felt a shudder make its way into her heart. Sudden fear had begun overwhelming her, and for a moment, she was sure that she might never see Daniel again.

Daniel tossed his mobile phone onto his bed, and in a fit of anger and frustration, he picked it up and hurled it against a wall. He had assured Megan only days before that Sarah would not allow her work to come between her, and her sister's wedding.

Daniel was annoyed, but it was his disappointment in her that entirely dominated him. When he picked up the broken pieces of his phone, the thought of never seeing her again had never felt as real, as it had at that very moment.

Claire was the eldest daughter, and the most level-headed and even-tempered of the entire Swanson clan. From an enormously young age, she buried her head in newspapers, and would change the television channel to any documentary or news channel she could find.

At the age of fifteen, Claire discovered a brand-new reality series that introduced her to a world of buying and selling exclusive and luxurious property.

From that moment on, it was all she could talk about, and all that intrigued her for years to come. She had no desire to meet boys, and later men, and was quite content to plunge herself head first into the dynamic, enthralling and glamorous world of realty.

Claire remained focused and career driven, and was determined to impress herself in the community, as the top realtor of Hazel Creek. Even though she regularly dated, she in no way at all, allowed her heart to manipulate or lessen her probability of success as a realtor.

She had spent five years at their local estate agency before she proudly opened the doors of her very own firm, Claire Swanson Properties. She was whole-heartedly devoted and committed to becoming Hazel Creek's largest listing agency, and thought very little of working extremely long, and tiring hours which left barely any time at all for her to fall in love.

She was the most ambitious of them all, and barely attended any family get-togethers other than Christmas and Easter.

Robert was the second youngest child of Thomas and Cindy Swanson. He grew up almost hiding behind his siblings. He was quiet and withdrawn, and very rarely enjoyed the spotlight. From the moment he had received his first doctor's play set as a little boy, he dreamed of becoming a doctor, and by the time he turned twenty-seven, he had received his degree and was working as a resident at The Hazel Creek Medical Centre.

He began dating a nursing student almost two years before, and by the time he had begun his residency, they had moved in together.

Benjamin Swanson was the oldest brother, and oldest

child of the entire Swanson clan. He loved designing and building things, and from a very young age, Thomas knew that he would someday, be an architect.

When Benjamin obtained his degree years later, he had no hesitation but to follow in his father's footsteps, and began working on the ranch where he would often formulate changes to existing structures on the farm or construct a new barn.

He would happily design or build a new shed from the ground up, or he would simply re-design Cindy's kitchen once it was outdated. They were a family of seven, but Thomas and Cindy Swanson knew from the very beginning that Sarah would be the child to stand out some day.

She turned out to be the child that refused to fade away into the background, and she grew up to be the most vocal of them all. Thomas Swanson was a tall and stocky man who was born and raised in Hazel Creek. He had been raised on the ranch he later inherited from his father.

Swanson Cattle Ranch had been in the Swanson family for generations before, and when Thomas met and married Cindy, a local bookstore owner, they were both eager to start a family on the ranch.

THE BOOKSTORE SERIES
Passage of Time – Book 1

Cindy adored the bookstore she opened shortly after she had graduated high school. As a young, single girl who had lost her parents a year before in a motor car accident, she found solitude and recluse in her bookstore, Fine Books.

She found peace and tranquility while surrounded by the stories so many authors were willing to share with her. She had converted a storage area upstairs to an apartment she lived in until she met and fell in love with Thomas.

Cindy continued to open the doors to Fine Books, and later converted the apartment upstairs to a safe reading area for the children of Hazel Creek. Sarah shared her mother's love for books and would often head straight for the little bookstore in the center of their beloved village, each chance she had.

She would beg Cindy to keep her from school some days, just so that she could spend a day at the bookstore.

She would carefully select a book, and rush upstairs to her very own little reading corner where she would spend all her free time reading anything and everything she could get her hands on, especially when new books were delivered.

She loved the smell of the pages that swept her up and out of the bookstore, before transporting her into a world she

Alice VL

could conjure up as she read on. She adored the feel of the turning of the pages, and she would often lose herself in the stories that were coming to life through the tips of her fingers.

It was not long after she had begun high school, that Sarah began writing her own stories in secret. She dreamed of someday telling her own stories and sending them out into the world. She found utter delight in the idea of holding her own book in her hands, and she never allowed herself to forget what Cindy once told her, "If you cannot find anything to read, my darling, you write it."

The Swansons were a functional, normal and happy family. They were extremely close-knit and supportive of one another, even through the darkest and most trying of moments.

Thomas and Cindy Swanson were loved and hugely respected by the entire Hazel Creek community. They were a part of a religion of the small town that embraced and treasured them.

Yet, Sarah could not discard feeling as though she was caged in and sheltered from the rest of the world. She was overwhelmingly conquered by an inexplicable urge to find her worth in the world, by crossing the borders of Hazel Creek and the safety she had known all her life.

She wanted to become an important person. She wanted to become someone others spoke fondly of. She wanted to write, and she wanted to write the very best books the world had ever seen. When she left for Queenstown shortly after graduating from high school, Sarah insisted that she would be gone no more than a year, and she swore to Daniel that she would return as someone wonderful, not too far in the not so distant future.

Queenstown was a city almost a thousand miles away from Hazel Creek. It was young, vibrant and bustling. There were trains and subways, apartments and malls. There were highways and bright night lights, all of which bewitched and captivated Sarah and the dreams she was hoping to chase and eventually, make her own reality.

It was often referred to as the city that never sleeps, and Sarah grew impatient to leave Hazel Creek behind her, and make her mark in the world, much to her parents' and Daniel's dismay.

Daniel Kingsley was deeply distressed by the fact that Sarah was so strong-minded in her quest to leave their village behind. He was eager to keep her close, and he was frantic for her to find contentment in their hometown, yet, it constantly appeared as though she was placing undue pressure upon herself to go faster than she was able to run.

He was about to complete his final year as a chartered accountant when Sarah excitedly shared her plans with him. Even though Daniel felt as though he may eventually lose her to the city, he unenthusiastically agreed to let her go in search of the magnificence she thought she needed, and so intensely sought.

"You're not coming back, Sarah. Once you're there, we'll hardly ever see you again."

"I am going to be gone for a year, Danny. One year! I won't be gone for longer than a year!" Daniel shook his head when he took her into his arms, and placed them firmly around her. He was much taller than she was, and quite the opposite in appearance.

Daniel's complexion was darker than Sarah's. His unruly, shadowy hair always seemed darker at night, but his eyes were so overwhelmingly blue, it almost seemed frosty and arctic at times. Sarah loved Daniel. She had fallen in love with the boy from the ranch next door when she was only a little girl. She would sit on the porch of the ranch she was born in, and watch him pass by each day, before he would disappear through the gates, and down the path of Kingsley's ranch.

She would stare out into the open fields in front of her, and dream of someday, becoming Daniel's girl. He was by far the most beautiful man she had ever seen, and when she finally entered her teen years, she was ecstatic and overjoyed when he fell in love with her.

She adored the boy she had met shortly after she had stepped into her grade one class for the very first time. She had met his sister Margie, who turned out to be the same age as she was, and who attended the same grade as she did. Before Simone had relocated to Hazel Creek the following year, Sarah and Margie became close friends almost from their first day at school.

When she met Daniel at Margie's seventh birthday party, Sarah knew that he was the boy she would marry someday. She fell in love with the schoolboy almost four years older than her, and although their brother Mark was closer to Sarah's age than Daniel was, it was Daniel who had stolen her heart from the very beginning.

Daniel had dated Kimberly Hossel on and off for most of his high school years. Sarah could never quite understand what it was that had drawn her to him, and when she ran into them on the beach, or at family get-togethers, she despised seeing Kimberly hang brazenly onto him, and onto every word he was saying.

When Sarah began her first day in grade ten, she was delighted to discover that Daniel and Kimberly had finally ended their rocky relationship. Daniel had begun his second year at college, and when she stumbled into him on the beach one Saturday night, she was thrilled that he had joined their diverse group of friends for a casual get-together, and that Kimberly was nowhere in sight.

They spent the evening fixing stares on one another, and by the time the evening had come to an end, Daniel had fallen head over heels in love with Sarah. It was when he dropped her off at home that night, that he kissed her for the very first time.

It was Sarah's first kiss, and when his lips gently touched hers, she knew it was the only lips that she ever wanted to feel against hers. After that evening, Daniel would rake up excuse after excuse to see her, and by the time her school year ended, they were inseparable.

"I am going to write books Daniel, and when I come back, you will be so proud of me!" She held him protectively against her before she rested her head on his chest. Sarah had graduated from high school only days before and turned eighteen only months earlier.

Daniel was in his final year at college, and was looking forward to entering the working world and starting out his life with Sarah. "I am already proud of you, Sè, you don't have to prove anything to me or to anyone else. You don't have to leave to show the world how good you are."

She gazed up at him, and smiled sadly when she noticed the raw melancholy in his eyes, "I do, Danny, I do. To me, to you, and to the world. I want to be proud of me, and deserving of you."

"What are you talking about, Sarah? You don't deserve any less than I do?"

"I want to be deserving of you, Danny, even if only to prove it to myself."

"You don't have to do this, you are wonderful. You are fabulous."

"Maybe someday you'll understand, Daniel. I love you so much, and I am going to miss you, but I must do this. I know there is something wonderful out there for me. Just please, don't forget me?" She leaned in closer and hugged him tightly. "I swear, Danny, you'll see my name in lights someday ..."

When Sarah boarded the flight to Queenstown, Daniel felt a gentle, nagging sensation that he was about to lose Sarah to the glamour of the city life, and to the world that was out there waiting for her. "Danny, I'll come back for holidays, I swear it. I'll come home every chance I get." She whispered as she clung desperately to him. For a moment, Sarah questioned all the plans she had made, and she wondered if leaving Daniel was worth hunting and chasing her dreams.

"Be safe out there, Sè ..." She retreated slightly, before she took his face into her hands, "Come with me, Danny, please come with me?"

He took her hands into his, before he wiped a lost tear that had rolled onto her cheek, "I can't, Sarah. I can't leave. The city is just not for me. Go do what you feel you need to do and come home. In the meantime, we'll call, email and you'll come visit, okay? And if I can, I'll visit you in the city. I know you, Sè, if you don't do this now, you'll spend the rest of your life regretting it, and blaming me for holding you back. I don't want you to leave but, I can't go with you." She nodded reluctantly, before she felt the confines of a hampering lump in her throat, forcing to swallow back on the tears she was desperate to hide from him.

As she stared into his wintry eyes, she felt an unexpected fear grab a hold of her heart, and for a moment, it paralyzed her entire being. For a split second, she was sure that she might never see him again. Sarah held him against her, and for a moment, she considered abandoning all her plans, and rather, remain in Hazel Creek and close to Daniel.

She slowly turned away from him, and made her way over to the checkpoint. Before she handed her ticket over, she turned back to Daniel. She smiled despondently when she saw him standing there. He was making a valiant effort to smile back at her, even though he could not shake the feeling that things were about to change for them.

He watched her hold her ticket and noticed that her hands had begun to tremble. He wanted to shout out for her to stay, that she could write her books right there beside him, but when he looked at her one more time, Daniel knew that he had to let her go. Sarah was missing something in her life.

He wasn't sure if it was the charisma of the city, or the lights she hoped to see her name in someday. Her dreams had kidnapped her and were relentlessly nudging her to go after whatever it was, she so desperately needed before she returned to him.

He raised his hand and waved at her while forcing a smile for her. Sarah smiled back at him, before she turned away, and disappeared into a corridor that would lead her out to the plane.

Daniel hurriedly made his way to the look-out point two flights of stairs up, and when he looked down onto the runway, he saw her hesitantly ascending the stairs to the plane that was about to take her a thousand miles away.

When she reached the top, she turned back to him, and when she noticed him standing on the other side of the glass window, she lifted her arm and waved to him. She wiped the tears that were escaping from her eyes, before she hurriedly boarded the plane without looking back again.

He caught a glimpse of the tears that had settled onto her cheeks, and could in no way at all, disguise the tears that had begun to shimmer in his own eyes. He wondered for a moment whether he shouldn't take a year off from Hazel Creek and join her in the city. Daniel shook his head and realized that the life Sarah was running after, was a life he could not imagine living in.

THE BOOKSTORE SERIES
Passage of Time – Book 1

"I love you, Sè ..." He whispered as her plane took off and disappeared into the sky.

THE BOOKSTORE SERIES
Passage of Time – Book 1

Alice VL

PART FOUR

Sarah laid quietly on his grave and thought back to Simone who she had seen only a few hours before returning to the ranch, and to her parents. She hadn't been home in twelve years, and she had barely spoken to her parents or her siblings. She had missed out on too many Easter gatherings, and far too many Christmas celebrations with her family.

She had skipped out on birthdays and she had shrugged off anniversaries as inconsequential milestones. It was never her intention to miss out on the holidays they treasured so dearly, or the moments she once cherished more than anything else in the world with her family, or with Daniel.

It was not for one moment her objective to be absent from these events, and it was never her goal to disregard the significance of these get-togethers, she just could never find the time to come home, even for only a weekend. She would exchange regular emails with her parents, while Sarah would catch up on news of her siblings through Cindy.

She would receive texts from her siblings on occasion, but she very rarely responded. She was always caught up in something more important, and would make a mental note to reply shortly, but she never did.

She would pre-program birthday or Christmas messages an entire year in advance, but she would never make the actual phone call to any of them. She had become totally engrossed in her jet-set lifestyle, so much so that she had failed to stop even for a moment, and reach out to her family.

Each year, she would swear to just another year, just one more year before she would return home to Hazel Creek. But as each year passed her by, a new, exciting opportunity would present itself, or a new project would come her way, one she could not disregard or say no to.

She travelled extensively, only it was never in the direction of Hazel Creek, or the man she had left behind. She repeatedly promised Daniel that she was obligated to complete one more project, one last task and commitment, before she was ready to return home to him.

When enough years had passed by, her parents no longer invited her home, and Daniel no longer asked her to come home to their village, and to him.

Her siblings stopped mailing photographs, and Cindy stopped making excuses for her absence or behavior. They had reluctantly accepted a reality where Sarah would not be home soon. Her priorities had changed.

Her self-importance had exploded, and her light was shining so brightly, it entirely blinded her. She was so caught up and engrossed in her success, that she no longer knew what it was that mattered to her. Her name was on most of the bestseller lists out there, and she loved the attention that came with her success.

Her picture was framed on the cover of magazines. Centre pages were persistently dedicated to her, and the interviews she loved giving out so freely, were featured in countless newspapers and online outlets. Sarah Swanson's name had landed amongst the stars, and there was no place left in her life, for the family and the man she had once, loved so dearly.

When Sarah finally returned to Hazel Creek, it had been almost two years since she had spoken to Daniel for the very last time. While lying on his cold grave, she thought back to their last phone call, and the very last conversation she was to have with him.

The tears continued to roll inexorably from her eyes, when she realized that she should have instinctively known that something was horribly wide of the mark with Daniel. She should have asked him what it was, and she should have heard it in his voice. She should have kept him on the phone for just a moment longer. She should have climbed into her car, and make the trip out to Hazel Creek.

There were so many things she should have done, instead, she did her best to stop loving him that day. "Danny?" She smiled when she heard his familiar voice on the other end of the call, the day she checked in with him for the very last time.

"Sarah, hey?"

"How are you, Danny?"

"I'm good, you?"

"I'm good, busy, but good."

"Yeah, you're always busy. I know this is probably a stupid question, but, are you coming home soon?"

"I want to. I'm working on that. These signings and tours,

you know?"

"Stop, Sarah! Just stop! You have had excuses from the moment you left. There is always something more important. There is always something else you must do first! Do you know how long it's been since you've been home?" Daniel had silenced her with his agitation, and Sarah was suddenly deeply embarrassed by the authenticity and realization that she had failed to return to Hazel Creek in twelve years.

As she stood listening to him, she could have sworn that she had only left the other day. When she quickly worked it out in her head, Sarah was horrified to discover that it had been more than a decade ago since she had last seen her parents, brothers and sisters, but more importantly, Daniel.

She had asked Daniel to wait for her, yet, she had never made the effort to return home for one visit or one single holiday. "Sarah, I don't expect your answers to be any different, so don't say anything. But, I don't want you to call me again. I can't do this with you anymore. You're always just another year away. You always just need one more year. You have one more quest and one more something to conquer. I've had to go on, Sarah, and I know you didn't really expect me to wait all these years? That would be crazy. I am pretty sure that you have moved on with your life over there as well. I've had to find my happiness, and I've met someone who I want to spend the rest of my life with. I've fallen in love and, I don't want you to call again, it's not fair to any of us."

Sarah swallowed back profusely on the tears that were threatening to silence her. She was sure that her heart had missed a beat when he told her that he had met someone else. As she stood holding the mobile phone in her hand, she quickly swabbed at the unanticipated tears that started plummeting down her cheeks.

"You've, you've met someone else?"

"I mean, Sarah? How long did you want me to wait? You check in once every two or three months. You never come home. You don't come home for Christmas. You just have so many excuses. I get it, Sarah. You've made it, you've found your wonderful. It's just, it's just not with me, or here in Hazel Creek, and I am okay with that. You've followed your dreams, you are someone! That's all you ever wanted, but now, Sè, you have to let me have my dreams too."

"Danny, this life, it's hard. There's never been anyone else, Danny. It's always been you. It will always be you. I want to come home, it's just …"

"It will never be enough, Sarah, I get that. Your accomplishments will never be enough for you. But I, I must go on. I've opened my own firm; do you even know that?"

"No, I didn't know that?"

"Yeah, I didn't think so. Sarah, I am so happy for you. I am glad that you are living your dream. But, you are missing out on so much. Your parents miss you. Your brothers and sisters miss you. Michael and Melissa are growing up, and you've never even met them? I don't get that? Family was once everything to you?"

She swallowed back, unsure of what to say next. "I just can't now, Danny, I can't. Not now …"   What she couldn't tell him was that she had been gone for so long, she no longer knew how to come home. She had missed out on so much, she no longer knew how to take back the life she had become a stranger to.

"Yeah, anyway Sarah. I must run. There's no reasoning with you. Please don't call me again. It's not that I don't want to hear from you, it's just not fair. It's not fair to the woman I plan on spending my life with. So, good luck. I hope you find whatever it is you're still looking for."

He ended the call before Sarah could respond. She placed the phone down on her desk, and stared blankly at the computer screen in front of her. It was the cover of her twenty eighth book staring back at her, and for a moment, she again questioned whether it was all worth it in the end.

She had accomplished all she had ever dreamed of, yet it never seemed to be enough. There was something inside of her that kept pushing her to test her boundaries and climb higher. She could not quite put her finger on what it was that was so fiercely nudging her, but she was powerless to silence the thunder that was raging underneath her feet all those years ago.

She gazed over at a photograph that Cindy had sent her only weeks before. It was a photograph of the entire Swanson clan, her parents, her brothers and sisters, their husbands and wives, and their children. They were all there, except for Sarah.

Her family back home had grown and changed, yet, her nieces and nephews have never met their aunt. The family she swore to stay close to had turned into strangers right before her eyes.

She lowered her head in shame, and was at once

disgusted by the fact that she had failed to appreciate the magnitude of family. She had not once considered that they might have stopped missing her, as they grew ardently accustomed to her endless excuses. Sarah burst into tears and covered her face with her hands. She had grown selfish and egotistical. She had become self-absorbed and difficult to love. She was estranged from the only family she will ever have, and the only man she would ever love.

Sarah had lived a lonely life for the past twelve years, while pressing herself to publish one book after another, outperforming all the goals she initially set for herself. She had barely slept through a night in years, and she could hardly remember when it was that she last heard her mother's voice.

She was at once angry at herself, and disappointed that so much time had passed. Sarah instantly and unsympathetically berated herself for allowing the increasing distance to come between them.

A thousand miles away from her, Daniel tossed the mobile phone onto his bed, and fell to his knees as he grabbed his head and tugged at his hair with both his hands. He loved Sarah, and even though he had lied to her, he had reluctantly kept his promise to wait for her. Yet, he could never tell her that he had never stopped loving her, and that he would wait for her, for an entire lifetime if he had to.

What he couldn't tell her was that he did wait an entire existence, but that his time had begun to run out. He sat down in front of his laptop, and half-heartedly, he typed out an email to her.

He told her that their thoughts and memories of one another were trapped, and forever lost in their once childhood dreams. He said that the years in between had stolen their promises and distorted the way his heart once sought hers out. He just couldn't wait anymore, he stopped dreaming of her a few years back.

He said that he had found someone new, and he hoarsely whispered that she was so much more like him. His heart had simply forgotten hers, but it was not entirely her fault. He said that perhaps too much time had passed, and too much distance had turned them into strangers to one another.

He reminded her of their foolish promises on a playground that no longer appealed to him, and that he could barely remember what they once swore to each other. He told her that they were merely the dreams of two innocent, foolish, starry-eyed, unwise and stupid children whose journeys had taken them away from one another, as was always an inevitable part of the universe's divine plan.

He again, asked her not to call him, and he begged her to forget their so-called childlike love, and carry on as though he never was, and they never were. He said that she should continue to see the world and run after her dreams, without him.

She should go in search of a love that would have to love her more than she could ever love him. He wanted her to settle in the little blue house a little way out of town, just as she had dreamed of as a child, where she could sit by a window, and dream of naming her babies, when she had grown tired of the city lights and bustling city streets.

He told her to forget him, just as he had forgotten her a long time ago. He sat staring at the letter he wrote, and wavered for only a single moment. He closed his eyes, and reminded himself that he had no other choice, but to lie to her one more time. He wanted her to forget. He could not bear the thought of her knowing the truth.

Yet, what he should have told her was, that the breaths he was taking in this world was fast running out, and that his new breaths would soon begin in a whole other world. One he didn't quite understand, and one he feared almost as much as losing her. He should have said that he could not stand to have her see him like that, and that he had never wanted to utter unkind words to her, or break his promise, or her heart.

Even if he had whispered it, he should have told her that his days were being counted, while hers would carry on long after he left. He never told her of his long fight, or how hard and bravely he fought just to be right there for her when she finally returned home to him. What he should have told her was that he had waited for her, and how ironically it had turned out that he had waited for her for his entire life.

He never meant to say goodbye with what seemed to be with no feeling at all, he never meant to betray the promises he clearly could remember, and once swore to her. He just could not give her a better reason for living his lie.

He didn't want to tell her about how he was painfully living their memories of so long ago, while he waited for the day his eyes would close one last time. He never wanted her to know what he already knew, that his fight was for nothing and that he was tired.

Alice VL

He was exhausted, and he was in pain. Even though he was never any good at playing it tough, it was their beautiful moments that he found his courage in.

What he should have told her was that while he was living in his own little world, one she would never know of, she would forever be the one that his heart would recognize.

What he should have told her was that she should listen more closely and hear what he isn't saying, as he tells her how he no longer loves her, and that he perhaps, never did.

That when the rain begins to fall, it was her he would stop to remember for a moment longer than he should. He should have told her how he wears his pain like a heavy coat around him, and that it is her face he sees, her smile he finds, and her eyes he searches for in everyone else.

What he should have told her was that he was about to die too young, and that death was about to steal all the remaining pages from their chapter, in a book that began almost a lifetime ago.

What he should have told her was that their story was really only about to begin, and that he would love her from the other side of the stars, especially when he hears her laughing in

Alice VL

the rain, or as she has her arms around another, or while she cradles her child in her arms.

What he should have told her was that even though she had pledged her heart to him a long time ago, she would be alright without him, because he would watch her, hold her, love her and miss her, from the other side.

Alice VL

It was months after her last phone call to Daniel, that she took the painting that she had begged the artist to paint for her on that busy city street, almost eleven months ago. She had placed it against the wall of her one bed-roomed apartment and gazed into the eyes that were searching hers. She sat on the floor and stared sorrowfully into the painting that brought her to her knees only moments before.

It had become dark, and as she wrapped her shawl around her, she stared at the man looking back at her. Her heart was not ready to let him go, and as though a jolt had entered her entire being, Sarah realized that her life in Queenstown suddenly meant nothing at all.

He was her story, and he was where her home would be. He was what she had dreamed of for most of her life, and Daniel was the only dream her heart had hunted and sought out.

When the sun peered through her bedroom window, Sarah realized that she had spent the entire night clinging to her love story, the only story that would ever matter to her, or make sense to her heart. It was time to go home.

It was time to leave the city lights behind her, and go home to the village she had left her heart in. It was time to turn her back on the dreams the city once promised it had in store for her, and go home to the little town that had given her all she ever needed. Yet, Sarah was deathly afraid and no longer knew how to return to a life she had left behind so many years before. She was terrified of what she might find, and she was horrified by the mere thought that Daniel might never love her again.

She packed her bags as fast as she could, and with trembling hands, she followed the sunrise back to Hazel Creek.

Alice VL

When Sarah entered the hair salon shortly after her phone call to Simone, she giggled softly when she noticed Simone fussing over one of her client's hair, but was at once elated to see her old friend again.

"Sim!" She shouted out before Simone swiftly turned around.

"Sarah, you're here? You actually are here!" Simone excitedly ran up to her and threw her arms around Sarah. Sarah smiled and held Simone snugly against her. "Go back there …" Simone pointed to a door while holding a scissors and brush in her hand. "It's my office, wait there for me. I am almost done with Mrs. Radcliffe …"

Sarah clutched her bag firmly against her, and hurriedly made her way into Simone's office. She sat down on the sofa and glanced around her. Simone's walls were cluttered with photographs of women sporting hairstyles Sarah never thought were possible, or were even worn.

She smiled sadly when she noticed all her framed certificates, and for a moment, she wondered how they had all grown up almost overnight. Again, Sarah could barely fathom how it was possible that so much time had passed. Simone strolled into her office almost ten minutes later, and found an empty seat next to Sarah. "I am so glad you're home, have you seen your parents yet?"

"No, I wanted to stop off here first. Maybe you could sort of prepare me, you know? I don't know much about much, you know? What do I need to know?"

Simone burst out laughing before she gave Sarah a quick rundown of her parents, brothers and sisters. They laughed out loud when Simone warned her of Claire's nose that was constantly stuck in the air, and how loud and unruly Melissa and Michael were.

"And you, Sim, how are you?"

"I am great, Sarah. As you can see, I have this fabulous place. I love it. I love the people and I adore my clients. Living the dream!" "Anyone special?"

"Well, maybe? We've been dating on and off for a year. He works for your dad, actually ..."

"Will I get to meet him?"

"Yeah, I mean, you are going home right?"

Alice VL

Sarah sighed before she lowered her head. "Yeah ..."

"How long are you here for, Sarah?" "I was thinking of coming home, for good. I mean, it's become pretty lonely on those crowded streets. I can write here. I can get a place in town, I just, I want to come home."

"Yeah, you should come home, you've been gone for far too long."

"I know, Simmy, but I swear, that was never the plan. It was never my intention to lose myself like that."

Sarah took Simone's hands into hers and gently squeezed them. "How is Danny?"

Simone at once freed her hands from Sarah's, and hurriedly got up. She stood staring at the photographs on her wall, unsure of what to say next. Sarah frowned at Simone's unexpected behavior.

"Sim?"

Simone shook her head, and without turning around, she began whispering hoarsely. "You really don't know? No-one ever told you? I mean, you honestly don't know?"

Sarah got up, and made her way over to Simone. She placed her hand on her shoulder, her heart stammering at an alarming rate in her chest. "Tell me what, Sim? What don't I know?"

She felt fear consume her entire body, as her hands began to gently shudder. Simone turned around to face her, and took Sarah's hands into hers, before she gently squeezed them. "He's gone, Sarah …"

Sarah frowned, and when she noticed the tears sparkle in Simone's eyes, she felt an untaught fear and dread entirely engulf her. "Where did he go?"

Simone lowered her head before she desperately wiped away the tears that had begun to roll carelessly down her cheeks.

"Where did he go, Sim?" She was almost shouting when she discovered the unexpected devastation on Simone's face.

"He, he, he died, Sè."

Sarah felt her legs grow weak underneath her as she stared at Simone in utter horror and total disbelief. She turned around, and hurriedly made her way back to the sofa in the corner of the room, her heart pounding as though it was about to climb out of her chest. She had barely reached the sofa when her legs gave in underneath her. She held onto to the couch, and stared out in front of her with overwhelming incredulity. Simone hurriedly made her way over to Sarah, and helped her back onto the couch.

"He didn't want you to know. He made us all swear, Sarah. It was his dying wish. He made us all swear when got sick that, that we never tell you. He didn't want you to see him like that?" She gazed up into Simone's eyes, while her own tears were threatening to trickle from hers.

"He was sick?"

"Yeah, he picked up a virus apparently when he was younger. I'm not sure exactly, maybe you should go and see Margie. Or Anabel? I don't really know the details, Sè?"

Sarah lowered her head before she burst into tears. Simone placed her arms around her, and held her firmly against her. It was for nothing. All she had ever hoped of becoming was for nothing. Her relentless search for her wonderful, no longer meant anything at all. Nothing she did, and nothing she dreamed of, had any meaning all of a sudden.

Through her tears, she stared questioningly at Simone,

Alice VL

who was holding onto her. "When?"

"About a year ago, please go and see Margie. Her store is just around the corner from here. You can't miss it. It has a Margaret Kingsley Event Planning sign right in front of it. You should go speak to her. They can tell you more."

"How could you not tell me, Sim?"

Simone lowered her head, and gently shook it. "I thought, I thought your parents would. I honestly didn't know that you didn't know?"

"I need to know what happened?"

"Sarah, please go and see Margie. I don't, I just don't want to say anything until you've seen your parents, or his family."

Sarah got up, and vigorously wiped the tears from her eyes. She felt the blood drain from her face, her heart hammering ruthlessly in her chest.

She smiled at Simone, and without uttering another word, she walked out of the salon. When she turned the corner of the road Margie's store was on, she at once caught a glimpse of the sign that was proudly displayed in front of Margie's store.

Sarah had barely composed herself before she walked in, desperate to control all the emotions that were wreaking havoc on her mind. When she opened the door, she at once recognized Margie who had begun displaying miniature wedding cakes that had more than likely, arrived only moments earlier.

She stood motionlessly for a moment, as she scrutinized the expressions on Margie's face. She was desperate to see something in her eyes, that would tell her that Daniel had not left, and that Simone had in fact, been mistaken.

As she watched her go about displaying her cakes, Sarah was convinced that she did not appear as a woman who had lost her brother almost a year ago. For an instant, Sarah was sure that the world would stop turning if Daniel was no longer a part of it, or at the very least, the earth would be slight moved off its axis.

There was no indication of either, and there was certainly nothing at all about Margie's disposition, that could confirm the cruel and heartless words Simone had uttered to her only moments before. "Can I help you?" Margie turned around and smiled at the stranger that had walked into her store.

It was painfully clear to Sarah that she did not recognize her, and that there was not so much as a hint of detection in her eyes. Sarah walked up to her, painfully aware of the fact that her eyes were red and swollen. "It's me, Margie, Sarah …"

Margaret frowned before her smile made way for an indignant expression on her face. She hurriedly turned around, anxious to avoid eye contact with Sarah, and uneasily continued to display the miniature cakes in the display cabinet. "What do you want?"

"I, I heard about Daniel, is it true?" She whispered hoarsely through the tears that were once again threatening to silence her.

Margie turned around to face her, and let out an enormous sigh before she lowered her head. When she looked up at Sarah again, Sarah knew by the look in Margie's eyes, that it was true.

"Go speak to my mom. She's at home."

"Everyone is telling me to speak to someone else, please Margie, just tell me!"

"You can't walk in here after all these years and expect us to just jump when you snap your fingers! Where have you been? Where were you when Daniel became ill? Where were you when he let out his final breath? No, Sarah, you don't get to do that!"

Sarah burst out crying and shuddered violently before she bowed her head in unreserved devastation and downright shame. The tears were unforgivingly streaming down her cheeks, and no matter how frantic she was to wipe them away, there seemed to be a never-ending supply.

It felt to her as though her heart had shattered into a million pieces. Her stomach turned with each quiver that went down her spine, each time she replayed Margie's words. "Go see my mom. I can't do this with you. You broke my brother's heart!"

"I didn't know, Margie, he never told me?" She whispered croakily through the river of tears that were streaming down her face.

"Yeah, he wanted to protect you. He didn't want to hurt you, even after you broke his heart, Sarah. You broke Daniel's heart! He waited for you, you know? He waited his whole life for you, Sarah."

"I, I loved him, Margie, I did love him. I didn't know? None of this makes sense?"

"Right, if you came home like you promised you would, you would have known! You were gone, Sarah. How long was it, twelve years? You never came back, not even once! He made so many plans to go visit you, but you were never ready for him to come? So, don't tell me you loved my brother! You didn't! He died, Sarah! He is dead! And if you ask me, he died of a broken heart!"

"I am so sorry ..."

Margie could barely hear Sarah through her violent sobbing. Sarah turned away from her, and hurriedly made her way back to her car. She climbed in, and placed her hands on the steering wheel, before she rested her head on her hands. She closed her eyes, desperate to cut off the tears that were incessantly flowing from her eyes. Margie was right.

She would have known that Daniel was ill, had she come home even once. Sarah cried out in anguish, and realized again, how self-centered and self-absorbed she had been. She had no right to claim that she loved Daniel, and there was nothing she could do to go back in time, and alter the course she had taken years before.

"I wish I could go back. God, please! Give me one more

last chance!" She shouted out through her tears as she sat weeping uncontrollably.

Alice VL

Barely twenty minutes later, Sarah drove in through the entrance of the Swanson Cattle Ranch. Not much seemed to have changed, but when she looked over at the ranch next door, she was horrified to discover that the Kingsleys ranch seemed cold, isolated and locked away behind the large gates she had never seen before.

She drove slowly as she desperately tried to swab away the tears that were flowing unremittingly from her eyes. She glanced around her, frantic to distract herself from the news she had received only a few moments ago. When she could finally see the farmhouse straight ahead of her, a fresh batch of tears began gushing mercilessly from her eyes. She had returned home.

The trees that lined the driveway seemed so much higher than they were before she had left. The farm seemed dissimilar, and the cattle hordes appeared to have doubled in size. The lawn was greener than she could remember, and her mother's rose garden was in full bloom.

She parked her car beneath the old oak tree that seemed as though it had aged a hundred years while she was away. She turned off the ignition and sat staring straight out in front of her. She wanted to go back to before.

Alice VL

The tempest inside of her was raging when she recalled how perfectly flawless she felt in Daniel's arms. She recklessly evoked the scent of his skin as every memory of a promise they once lived, came flooding back to her. Almost like a song she was once besotted with, but hadn't heard in far too many years, and how the lyrics remained imprinted in her soul as she memorized each word.

She wanted to go back to before, and grab his hands while she shamelessly begged him to go away with her. To run away. To go too far. Just for one more last chance, to go back to before.

Before she was someone important, and before he left their world. To before they knew too much and felt too little. To when they could still effortlessly function on love and desire alone. She wanted one more last chance to evoke the she, she once was, the she, she was with him.

She wanted to go back, far away to a time when they were a them. To let go of their now, and forget how they grew up and lost their magic. To before their lights were so cruelly turned down. To a time when no-one else mattered, and not much else was real.

Alice VL

To when their bodies spoke so much louder and so much clearer than their voices did. She wanted to go so far back to when their hearts dissolved into their souls, just like they once did.

She wanted to go back to before life snuffed him out, and stole their passionate flames. She wanted to sit with him and hold his hand tightly into hers. She wanted to drown in the puddles of his arctic and wintry eyes.

She wanted to splash around on the shore with him and gaze up at the stars as they counted almost everyone. She wanted to dream the same dream he once did, before life stepped in, and flung them into separate and untaught terrains.

She wanted to go back just for one more last chance, and forget that she became someone else he had hardly recognized. She wanted to forget that she pledged her heart to the city. For one night, she wanted to be free to unreservedly, love him again.

She wanted to whisper how her heart still sought him out, and how her body still craved his. She wanted to step back into, and shamelessly linger in a moment she once thought she would never lose.

"One more last chance, Dear God. Just one more, last

chance. I beg of you ..." She continuously cried out, and begged through her crushing tears.

She was still hopelessly caught up in her negotiations with the universe when she noticed Thomas approach her. He was her father, but he looked different. Perhaps older, and perhaps, a little sadder. It felt as though her trampled heart would barely be able to survive the moment she was about to see her beloved father again after all the years. The sun had disappeared behind the clouds, and the wind had begun to howl harshly around her. She climbed out of her car, and ran into her father's arms where she sobbed bitterly into his chest.

"Daddy ..." Thomas Swanson placed his arms around his daughter, and held her protectively against him. He swallowed back on the tears he was sure were about to escape through his eyes, and for a single moment, he was sure that he was dreaming.

"You're home? Why didn't you tell us you were coming home?" He was ecstatic to hold her in his arms again, but devastated that her world had appeared to fall apart around her. She had barely lifted her eyes when she heard her mother's voice echo in the distance.

"Sarah! Sarah!" She retreated slightly before she peeked

over her father's shoulders. When Cindy reached them, she placed her arms around Thomas and Sarah, and held desolately onto them.

"Mommy …" Sarah whispered before she began sobbing again.

"Baby? What happened? Why didn't you let us know you were coming home?" Cindy was at once horrified by the state she found her daughter in. Sarah erupted into a violent shudder before Thomas and Cindy led her into the farmhouse.

When they reached the dining room, Thomas hurriedly pulled out a chair, and helped Sarah into it. She swabbed irritatingly at the tears that refused to dry up any time soon. "Daniel? Is it true?" She whispered hoarsely before Cindy sat down on an empty seat beside her.

Thomas turned away, and despondently made his way to the kitchen. He knew that the moment would come that Sarah would discover the truth about Daniel. He knew that she would find out someday, and come home for answers.

Thomas not once agreed with Daniel when he frantically begged them never to tell Sarah, and when he saw the utter desolation in his eyes, he suddenly wished he had disregarded

Daniel's wishes, and ordered Sarah to come home. "He didn't want you to know, he thought he was protecting you …"

She slammed her fists into the dining room table before she turned to look her mother in the eye. "Protect me? Protect me? From what?"

"Honey, he never thought you'd come back here. He just never wanted you to leave everything behind for him, for this."

"I did, I did come back. I said I would! You mommy, you should have known that I'd come home! You should have told me he was sick. You should have given me my one last chance to come home and be here for him. You should have given me my one last chance to say goodbye to him. I lost that! I have nothing, mother! You, dad and Daniel stole time from me! I was gone for too long, mommy, you should have told me! Sim says he was sick? That he suffered?"

"Honey, he suffered for such a long time. He didn't want you to see him like that. And after all these years, we just didn't think? We thought that Danny was no longer in your plans? He said that you broke up a few years before?"

"Danny has always been in my plans! Always, mom, always! And he broke up with me! He told me he found someone else! He said he couldn't wait for me anymore!" She rested her head in her hands, as she continued to sob viciously. She turned her head, and stared blankly at her mother, "What happened? How did he get sick?" She had only just managed to ask her mother over the ever-restricting lump in her throat.

"Oh baby, the doctors are fairly sure that he picked up a virus when they left for Spain back in 1986. Their last trip to Anabel's mother before she passed away, do you remember? It was just after you and Daniel began dating. The doctors were of the opinion that the virus lay dormant for all these years. They think that, well, they think that it had flared up for no reason at all, and began to attack his heart without warning. There were no symptoms before, nothing to indicate that something was wrong? But, when it surfaced, it took too long to diagnose …"

She paused to take in a deep breath. "During Christmas of 1997, he developed a fever, and it took them almost two years to diagnose and discover that it was a virus that was, that was aggressively attacking his heart. There was nothing they could do, honey. It was too late for a heart transplant. There was just nothing they could do, and there was no way they could have diagnosed it sooner."

She stared at her mother in disbelief. Sarah angrily

dabbed at the tears that had continued to gush from her eyes.

"So, if they had never gone to Spain, this would never have happened?" Cindy nodded her head before she turned away from Sarah.

"He picked up a virus in another country just to come home and die? And nobody tells me a damn thing! It was not your decision to make, mother! It was not yours, dad's or Daniel's!" Sarah stood up before she hurled her chair into the corner of the dining room.

"Where is he?" Cindy walked over to Sarah who had become hysterical. "Where is he, mother?" She yelled out at the top of her voice.

"He's, he's buried at the Hazel Creek Cemetery."

She grabbed her bag and her keys, before she hurriedly made her way back to her car. "Sarah!" Cindy followed her out to her car, and when she reached Sarah, Cindy grabbed firmly onto her arm, "Sarah, you're too upset to drive. Megan is coming over with the kids later, why don't you let her drive you?"

"No! I have to be where he is! Alone!" She freed herself from Cindy's grip, before she slid into the driver's seat, and started her car. She glared furiously over at Cindy, before she pulled away, and as though in a daze, she made her way to the cemetery.

Alice VL

THE BOOKSTORE SERIES
Passage of Time – Book 1

While Sarah lay curled up in a bundle on his grave, she once again replayed their last conversation. She criticized herself for leaving him, and she hated herself for allowing twelve years to pass by before she came home.

She closed her eyes and desperately tried to remember what his voice sounded like. She could in no way at all, discard the crackle she heard in his voice, when he told her not to call him again.

She should have known that he was saying so much more than what she was hearing. His voice had pleaded with her, while his tone had scolded her, all at the same time.

Daniel Kingsley was the boy she had left behind, but he was always the man she thought she would come back to, and start her forever with someday.

In all the years that she had been gone, she stubbornly dreamed of the day they would own their own ranch, while she wrote her stories in her mother's bookstore.

Her dreams of a life with Daniel had never changed, yet, the passage of time had turned against her. It had allowed the bright lights and city nights to seduce her, while it continued to blatantly tick by, second by second.

Alice VL

It gave her no warning. There was no indication that it would soon run out for her, and for Daniel. It never once alerted her of the fact that while she was away, the passage of time had turned against Daniel, and ultimately, turned against her. It had tricked her into believing that there was more time, almost as though it would never run out.

It was later than she thought. She placed her hands over the grass that was neatly cut and trimmed, and she gently ran her fingers across them. She wondered if his soul could feel her, and she wondered if he perhaps knew how she would spurn herself for leaving him.

She hated the fact that he had fallen ill and died. She cursed the fact that she never knew, and again, she scolded herself for turning her back on all that had ever mattered to her. "If I could go back, Danny …" She cried out through her sorrowful tears as she clutched at the grass straws below her.

It had begun to rain, and Sarah no longer knew if it was her tears or the rain that had begun drowning her. She could almost not breathe, and she was sure that her heart could not stand the crushing of her heart and the shattering of her soul that she was so sure she could physically feel.

Alice VL

"I wish I could go back. I wish I could go back …" She whispered softly before the thunder and lightning began crashing down around her. Sarah did not care that a storm had begun to entirely surround and engulf her. The sun had wholly disappeared, and the clouds had grown heavy and sinister above her.

The rain came crashing down on her, while angry flashes of lightning began lighting up the sky above her. She closed her eyes and thought back to the day they left for Spain. It was shortly before Christmas, and for some reason, Sarah could clearly remember that it was the 17th day of December.

The entire Kingsley family were about to board a ship to visit Anabel's family in Galicia, for one last visit. Daniel was only twenty years old, and although he was excited to see his grandparents, he was reluctant to leave Sarah behind.

They had begun dating only a short while earlier, and had spent much of their free time together, where Daniel would regularly join her in the bookstore after school. Sarah was hesitant to see him leave, and when they said goodbye to one another at the docks, she was defeated by an unexpected and unforeseen urge to plead with him to stay.

She laid replaying each moment before he boarded the ship, and she realized at once that she must have known instinctively that Daniel should never have boarded that ship to Spain.

"I don't want you to go, Danny …" She pleaded with him when he pressed her firmly against him.

"I don't want to go, but this will be the last time I get to see my grandmother, Sè …"

"I know, Danny, I just, I'm going to miss you. I am going to miss you so much …" He kissed her gently before he joined his parents and boarded The Alicia.

"He left that day to begin dying …" She whispered sadly as she lay in the puddle of water on top of his grave. "I wish I could go back. I wish I could stop you from leaving. I wish I could go back …"

She whispered over and over before she yelled out at the top of her voice in anger and desolation, "You can't take him from me! I want another chance! I want my do-over!"

She sat up straight, and looked up into the sky, before she yelled out through her desperate tears. "I want to go back to before!" She was suddenly blinded by lightning that she was sure had crashed down right beside her.

The thunderous roars were deafening her, and the rain had completely blinded her, and drowned out everything around her. She felt eerie warmth enter her entire being, and when she closed her eyes, darkness had wholly surrounded her, and swallowed her up.

She fell back onto his grave, where she lay motionlessly, almost as though she was slipping into a deep sleep. She placed her hands on the ground below her, before the darkness entirely consumed her, "I want to be where you are ..."

Alice VL

PART FIVE

"Sarah, Sarah, wake up!" Sarah opened her sleepy eyes and peered groggily at Benjamin who was standing in her doorway.

"Ben?" She whispered in confusion as she slowly sat up in bed, before she hurriedly glanced around her. "Ben, what are you doing here? You look so ... young?"

"Come on, Sarah. You're going to be late for school! Mom wants me to take you, so please, I cannot be late for class this morning." Sarah frowned before she burst out into a nervous laughter. As though in one motion, she leaped from her bed and fell into her older brother's arms.

"I've missed you, big brother ..." She whispered in his ear before she squeezed him tightly.

"Are you feeling alright?" He stepped back slightly, and gazed apprehensively at her. Sarah grimaced, and realized once again how it seemed as though he hadn't aged one single minute.

Alice VL

"Come on, Sarah, you have ten minutes, then I'm leaving, with or without you!" He agitatedly turned away from her before he hurriedly made his way downstairs.

"Mom!" Sarah glowered once again and smiled when she recognized Claire's voice echoing down the passage. "Megan won't give me back my sneakers!"

Sarah stood in the doorway, and for a moment, she felt entirely disoriented. It suddenly made no sense to her why Claire and Megan, who had grown up and had left home years before, would be arguing about sneakers in their childhood home.

"Megan! Give back your sister's sneakers now! Don't let me come up there!"

"Mom! She said I could wear them!" Megan yelled back as she hurriedly ran down the stairs. Claire followed closely behind her as they pushed each other out the way, before rushing into the kitchen.

Sarah stood in silence at the scene that had played out right in front of her only moments earlier. She could have sworn that they were replaying scenes from their teen years, and it felt like a thousand years ago.

While listening to them continue yelling at one another, Sarah was convinced that she was stuck in a vivid dream, only one she had recognized, and one she had lived, once before.

She had only just turned to make her way back into her bedroom, when she heard Robert's voice behind her, "Good morning, Sissy. Ben is about to leave, you better hurry, or you'll walk again!"

Sarah burst out crying and flung her arms around Robert, the brother who appeared to be in his third year of medical studies.

"Sarah?"

Robert placed his arms around her and tapped her gently. She retreated slightly, before she hurriedly wiped her tears, and smiled sadly at the brother she hadn't seen in years.

"You okay?"

"Yeah, I just, you guys are all here?" She whispered croakily through the tears that laid squelchy on her face.

"Where else would we be? Come on, you know how Ben gets?" Robert smiled before he turned away from her.

Alice VL

"Wait!" She grabbed him from behind and turned him around to face her.

"How old am I?"

"Sarah, what's the matter with you?"

"Please Robbie, what year are we in?"

You are sixteen Sarah and it is 1986! You know that! What's the matter with you?"

Her eyes grew wider and her mouth hung open. She was sixteen again. In her dream, she was back in the year 1986. The same year she became Daniel's girlfriend.

She was dreaming of a time when life had so much in store for her. She was wholly engrossed in a dream when life seemed so much simpler, and when all she cared about was writing her stories and loving Daniel.

"Yeah, I was just asking. You see Robbie, I think I might be dreaming, and that this is all a dream, and I just want to be here, like I'm really here, you know?" Robert shook his head, before he hurriedly made his way downstairs.

Sarah smiled sadly as she made her way back into her

bedroom, almost as though she was wandering through a foggy mist. She sat down on the edge of her bed and glanced around her bedroom.

It was all as it was before, when she was a teenager and when she was sixteen years old. She gazed at each poster against her wall, and she smiled at all the rock stars looking back at her. She hurriedly opened the drawer next to her bed, and quickly took out her journal. When she paged through, she realized that her last entry was in June 1986. She quickly grabbed her school bag, and pulled out her school books. She was desperate to find a date, and when she heard Cindy call for her, she carefully placed the books back into her bag, and rushed into the bathroom.

She stood staring at her reflection in the mirror. It felt as though the girl looking back at her was a total stranger. The girl staring back at her was a young, vibrant and carefree girl who was barely sixteen years old.

She opened the cold-water tap, and quickly splashed her face with ice cold water. When she looked up again, it was the same young girl mimicking her every move. "Damn, this is quite a dream …"

She brushed her teeth, and quickly tied her hair into a ponytail. She ran back into her bedroom, and promptly threw on a pair of jeans and a sweater before she grabbed her school bag. "Daniel!"

It had suddenly dawned on her that Daniel had not yet died, and that he was still the boy at the ranch next door. When she breathlessly reached the kitchen, she smiled broadly when she saw her parents and all her siblings around the kitchen table.

It had been far too long for Sarah, and as she stood staring at them, listening to their squabbles, she dabbed at a lost tear that had once again, rolled carelessly down her cheek.

"What's the matter, Sarah?" Thomas was at once concerned by the expression on Sarah's face. She smiled before she quickly slid in beside Benjamin.

"Nothing, daddy ..."

"Sarah, you are not going to make me late. You have five minutes ..." Benjamin was at once agitated by Sarah's passiveness.

"I'll just have coffee. Can we stop off at Daniel's? She whispered before she poured herself a cup of coffee.

THE BOOKSTORE SERIES
Passage of Time – Book 1

"I don't have time, Sarah."

"Never mind, I'll walk to school. I need to see Daniel …"

"You can see him after school, Sarah. It's too far to walk, and you'll be late. Besides, Daniel has class this morning, so you might see him for a few minutes before he leaves for class. Also, don't forget that it's your turn to shelve the returns at the bookstore today …" Cindy took a bite of her toast, and stared curiously at her youngest daughter.

"I must see him, mom! I'll be at the bookstore, I promise." She rose to her feet and placed her cup of coffee back down on the kitchen table. "That's if, I don't wake up before then …" She whispered inaudibly before she smiled, and turned away from the Swanson clan.

Just as she was about to leave the kitchen, she turned back to the family she had yearned for, with her entire heart. "I, I love you guys, all of you …" She whispered croakily before she waved and ran out the front door.   Thomas frowned, and could in no way at all, shake the feeling that all was not well with Sarah.

Alice VL

Sarah fearfully made her way down the road that led to the Kingsley ranch. She was intensely afraid of seeing Daniel again, but excited that she was dreaming about him again for the very first time since she heard that he had died.

She was anxious to reach him, and when she saw the big white house on the hill, she was sure that her heart was about to hammer from her chest. She opened the gate that would place her on a familiar, soothing path that would lead her right up to his front porch. When she reached the terrace, she at once recognized the swing they had sat on together almost a hundred times before.

She smiled sadly when she thought back to the hundreds of moments they sat there for the first time as children, and then again late at night, as teenagers. She nervously made her way to the front door, and was at once aware of voices that were coming through from the other side of the walls.

Sarah knocked softly and was almost at once greeted by Margie's familiar face. She had never noticed before how beautiful Margie was. She gazed at her and was once again reminded of their meeting at the store only the day before. Sarah was sad to realize how Daniel's death had taken a toll on her, and how Margie had aged at an alarming rate after he had died.

Alice VL

"Hi Sè, come on in!"

Sarah smiled and quickly made her way into the Kingsley home. "He's in his bedroom …"

"Thank you …" She smiled before she turned away.

"Margie, Daniel is lucky to have you." Sarah whispered and almost as though she was tiptoeing, she made her way down the hall.

When she reached his closed bedroom door, she hesitated before she knocked gently. Her entire body had begun to quiver, and her hands were violently shuddering as she waited to hear his voice.

"Come in!"

When she heard his voice, she was sure that her heart was about to leap right out of her chest. She could not lift her arms to open the door, and she was sure that her legs were about to give way underneath her. For a moment, her stomach turned and into the very core of her, she felt a jolt rush through her.

"Sarah?" He had opened the door, and was standing right in front of her. "Why are you just standing there? Come on in …" He turned away from her, and quickly made his way back to his desk.

Sarah could barely move. It felt to her as though her entire world had stood still. She was once again sure that Daniel Kingsley was the only man she could ever love, and that her dream had reached her just in time. She thought back to the world outside of her dream, and she thought back to the reality of his illness, and his death. Her heart felt as though it would shatter by the very thought, and she was certain she could almost hear it splinter into a thousand pieces.

The pain that had begun to consume her entirely overwhelmed her, almost as though her soul was throbbing from deep inside of her. She lowered her head into her hands before she burst out crying.

Daniel looked up and noticed that she hadn't moved. She was sobbing bitterly in her hands, and it suddenly scared him almost to death to see her in such an inexplicable state. As if in one motion, he had bolted from his seat and rushed over to her. "Sarah?" He whispered raucously when he placed his arms around her. She rested her head on his chest and placed her arms firmly around him. "What happened, Sè?"

He led her into his bedroom, before he closed his

bedroom door behind them. He sat her down on his bed, moments before he sat down beside her. He held her protectively against him, and left her to cry in his arms. When her shuddering and sobbing began to subside, she looked up, and gazed into his eyes. "I never thought I'd see you again …" She whispered huskily, while her body continued quivering slightly.

"What, what are you talking about, Sarah?"

She gently shook her head and quickly wiped the endless supply of tears from her eyes. "I just, I am so glad to see you, Danny …"

"Hey, what's going on, Sè?" He took her hands into his, and nervously squeezed them. "I'm not going anywhere …"

She smiled when she noticed the tenderness in his eyes. "But you are, Danny. You're going to be gone someday, not too long from now, you're going to be gone."

"Sarah, I don't know what's going on, but I swear, I'm not going anywhere!"

She bowed her head, before she again, swabbed at the tears that had continued to roll onto her cheeks. "What day is it today, Daniel?"

Daniel frowned, and hesitated for a moment. "June 16th?"

She smiled and realized that they had not yet been on their trip, and that Daniel had not yet picked up the virus that would ultimately take his life. He had not yet been exposed to the very dread of the reality that had begun to haunt her.

"Why do you ask?"

"Just asking …" She paused, before she leaned closer.

"Danny, you must listen to me, please. I know I sound crazy, and I know I seem crazier than anything you'll ever understand, but, if this is just a dream, I might not sound as foolish as I think I would …" She paused when she considered her words for a moment. "December, in 1997, something really bad is going to happen, and, and it all starts with your trip to Spain this year. You can't go, you have to listen to me, Danny."

Daniel frowned as he stared blankly at Sarah. "That's eleven years from now?"

She nodded and quickly turned away when she noticed the confusion in his eyes.

"You can't possibly know what's going to happen eleven

years from now?"

"Danny, it starts with your holiday at the end of the year. You can't go! You are going to pick up a virus. And in December 1997, you are going to get really sick. It will be bad, and you'll be sick for three years, and then, then you're going to die. In March of 2000, you'll, you're going to die, Danny, and you ... I won't know until a year later ..."

Daniel frowned and stood up before he made his way over to his bedroom window. He ran his fingers through his hair, before he turned back to her. Sarah was sure that he had believed her, after all, it was a dream and one she could manipulate any way she wanted.

"I don't know what's going on with you, Sarah? This trip is a family reunion. Our last visit with my grandmother. You are sounding like a crazy person?"

Sarah got up and slowly made her way over to Daniel. She gently touched his face, while gazing into his frosty, captivating eyes. "Danny, please, I am begging you. If that's all you ever do, don't go on that trip. Don't go, please!" She grabbed onto him with both her hands as she pleaded and begged Daniel to believe her.

"Stop, Sarah! Just stop! This is crazy!"

Sarah despondently lowered her head when she realized how fanatical and foolish she sounded. "I know, but Danny, this is crazy to me too. Yesterday, I was thirty-one years old, and today, I am sixteen again. I fell asleep on your grave last night, and woke up to this? You never told me, Danny, and you wouldn't let anyone tell me you were sick. You just died, without me?"

"Sarah, you are making no sense!" Daniel grabbed her by her shoulders, and gently shook her.

"Margie, she is going to be a wedding planner; did you know that? Did you even know that that is what she is dreaming of? And Mark, Mark is going to be a lawyer and you, Danny, you will be a CA at your own firm, four years before you die."

"Yes, Sarah, that is what I am studying for, and that is what Mark is in his final year of. But, you are wrong about Margaret. She doesn't know what she wants yet. Besides, my dad will never approve of her becoming some or other party planner?"

"Then, let's go ask her!" Sarah yelled out at the top of her voice as her frustration grew.

"Fine!" He grabbed Sarah by her arm, and yanked open his bedroom door.

"Margie!" He yelled down the hallway as Sarah remained silent.

"What?" Margie yelled back, irritated by Daniel's impatience.

"What do you want to be when you grow up?"

"Nothing!" She yelled back in anger and frustration before she appeared in front of Daniel and Sarah.

"Margie, aren't you dreaming of becoming a wedding planner someday?" Margie's eyes grew bigger before she frowned and glared at Sarah. "No?"

Sarah lowered her head, when she realized that Margie was her only chance to prove to Daniel that she was telling the truth.

"See!" Daniel turned to Sarah, and smiled before Margie hurriedly slipped away, and disappeared into her bedroom.

"Danny, I don't care what Margie says. That is how it's going to end, you'll see, and when she is a wedding planner, it will be too late. By the time you remember this conversation someday, it will be too late! When you remember all of this, it will be too late!" Sarah yelled out before she ran down the hall, and out of the front door of the Kingsley home.

PART SIX

"Sarah! Wait up!"

Sarah turned around to find Simone running to catch up to her. She smiled when she saw her childhood friend, and she couldn't help but wonder how it was that they all turned out living such separate lives.

When Simone reached her, Sarah threw her arms around her and hugged her tightly. "I've missed you ..." Sarah whispered, holding onto her friend.

"Sè, are you okay?"

"Yeah, it's just, we're going to grow up soon, and we're all going to go our separate ways ..."

"No, we won't, you'll see ..."

Sarah took Simone's hand as they strolled along the corridor just as their first school bell was about to ring.

"Sarah!"

Alice VL

She hastily turned around when she heard Margie's voice behind her.

"You can't tell Daniel about what you heard. Where did you hear it anyway?"

Sarah frowned and stared at a breathless Margie. "Hear what?"

"You know? The whole wedding planning thing ..."

"So, it's true? I'm not going crazy?"

"You can't tell them. My dad will go nuts when he finds out that I don't want to teach. Please, Sarah, I don't know who told you, but you can't tell anyone!" Margie grew increasingly desperate when she pleaded with Sarah.

Sarah grabbed her hands, and stared at Margie in utter disbelief, "You have to tell Daniel! You don't understand, you have to, Margie. His life, you telling him, you must tell him! It might save his life!"

"You're hurting me, Sarah ..."

Sarah let go of her hands before she grabbed her by her shoulders, "You have to tell Daniel!" She yelled out at the top of her voice.

Margie was suddenly overcome by fear, when she noticed the deranged expression in Sarah's eyes. "No. What's the matter with you? I will deny it, Sarah, so just leave it! Drop it!" She turned away, and hurriedly made her way into her their classroom.

Simone frowned when she stared at Sarah who had turned ashen all of a sudden. "Sarah, what was that all about?"

Sarah lowered her head before she turned to Simone who in turn, frowned when she noticed the tears flickering in Sarah's eyes. "What's going on with you?" Simone was desperate to determine what it was that had so tremendously upset her best friend.

"It's of no use, Sim, nobody believes me …" Her voice trailed off when a restricting lump in her throat made its appearance, once again.

"Tell me, Sè …"

She took Simone's hand and gently squeezed it. "Not here. Meet me at the bookstore this afternoon, okay?"

"Sure …"

Sarah smiled before she made her way into their first class of the morning.

When their bell rang for the first break of their school day, Sarah quickly ran out to the pavilion after grabbing a book she had kept in her school bag. She smiled when she read the title, "The Weeping Prince," and remembered that it was a book she had begun to read, but could not quite remember finishing.

When she reached the pavilion on the sports field, she was relieved to notice that she was alone, and away from the chatter and bustling of the rest of the students. She quickly climbed a dozen steps, and sat down before she opened the book exactly where she had left off all those years ago.

She had barely begun to read, when Daniel's familiar voice startled her. "Sarah? Simone said I could find you here …"

"You're not allowed to be here, what are you doing here?"

Daniel swiftly climbed the steps towards her and sat down beside her. He took her hand into his, and gently squeezed it, "I just wanted to say sorry about this morning."

Sarah's heart broke out into a flutter, before she smiled

excitedly at him. "You believe me?"

He lowered his head and gently kissed her hand. "I think you believe it, but I think maybe, just maybe you might have dreamed it all?" He peered up at her and gazed into her emerald green eyes.

Sarah turned away from him, and for a moment, she was not sure what was real and what never was. She could very well be dreaming, but she knew, from the innermost core of her, that he had died. In her world, the real world that he too belongs to, he had died.

She had no idea why she was dreaming such a vivid and on-going dream. She had no clue why her dreams had taken her back to that specific year, but she knew that she had to try and save him, even if only in her dream.

She had nothing much left to lose, if all she was living in was a dream. "Danny, I don't know whether it's possible to dream in a dream. But, what I do know is that I'm going to make the biggest mistake of my life someday. I am going to leave Hazel Creek, and try to be better and do better. I won't know about your illness, and I won't come back until after. I wish I could change that. I wish I could change and alter my path and my choices, but all I can do right now, is try and change yours."

"Sarah, sometimes we think that our dreams appear to us as warnings, but they're not. They are just dreams. We have plans you and I. You will never leave Hazel Creek. I know you."

"Daniel! Stop it! Ask my mother. As a little girl, I dreamed of going to the city and becoming a famous writer. Our plans will mean nothing because you, you will be dead! You are going to get sick and die. And you can stop it! You can change it, but you won't listen to me!"

He let go of her hand, and lowered his head, unable to look her in the eye. He sighed, before he turned back to face her. "I know you believe what you think will happen. But, unless someone gave you some of their magic, you can't predict the future, Sarah. I'm not going to get sick. I've never been sick a day in my life, Sarah?"

Sarah rose to her feet, and closed her book in anger. "The bell is going to ring! I have to go back to class!"

Daniel got up and grabbed her before she turned away from him. "I love you, Sè. I love that you worry about me, but I will never leave you. You'll see …"

Alice VL

"Yeah, and when you get sick, Danny, just know that no-one can save you, because it will be too late!"

Daniel felt a shudder rush through his heart when he heard the conviction in her voice. For a moment, he wondered if he should believe her, or at the very least, believe that she believes he will die. While watching her run back to her class, he could not discard the feeling of uneasiness that had suddenly, entirely overwhelmed him.

When the last school bell of the day rang, Sarah rushed out of her classroom, and quickly dashed down the road that led her to her mother's bookstore. When she opened the old, heavy wooden doors to Fine Books, she was again reminded of how magical her mother's bookstore felt to her. Each time she would walk through that door, she was sure she was stepping into a world of fascination.

She loved the smell, she loved the silence and she fully embraced the serenity she found as she walked through the rows and rows of books. Some new, and recently bought, and some that were hundreds of years old.

Sarah would keep what she called the special books in a corner somewhere, away from the public almost as though they were a hidden treasure. She would tell Sarah that the books that were leather bound and frail, were special, and had more than just stories to tell. She hated the idea that some stranger might come across them, and page through their brittle pages, with their unwashed hands.

"Hey mommy …"

"Hello, my girl …"

Sarah smiled sadly before she made her way around the counter to where her mother was standing.

"Are you alright, my lovey?"

Sarah nodded when her lower lip began to quiver. She could not swallow back on the tears that had begun to escape through the hampering lump in her throat, and when they began shimmering in her eyes, Cindy took Sarah's hands into hers. "What's wrong, my girl?"

She swallowed back before she quickly wiped the tears that were threatening to bucket from her eyes. "I, I don't want to talk about it, mommy. Sim is coming to help me later on; can I just hide out in my reading corner for a bit?"

"Of course, baby. I've left you a sandwich. Here, I got this book in the mail the other day, and I thought you might want to read it. It was very special to my mother. I searched everywhere for it, and when I found it, I knew you must have it."

Cindy handed Sarah a bulky, leather bound book that appeared scuffed and worn. She rubbed her hand over the binder, and smiled when she noticed the tiny ribbon around it. At that very moment, Sarah was sure she had seen that book before, and that her mother had given it to her once before.

She knew that she had begun reading it many years before, and she could clearly remember leaving it hidden on a shelf in her reading corner. She grimaced as she gazed at the title that was branded deep into the cover, 'The Passage of Time.' When she turned the book over, she stood as though frozen in time when she read the words carved into the leather binding,

'For one moment in time, for one call of the heart and the mind to the soul, time is nothing. When the soul agrees that there might have been a fault in the stars, the heart, the mind and the soul will come together, and alter one moment in time.'

She began trembling slightly when she remembered reading those exact same words once before. Years before, when she believed in the magic of words. When she believed in the power of story book pages, and how she was convinced that her mother's bookstore could make time stand still.

"Is this it? Can this be?" She whispered softly as she stood staring at the book.

"Can what be?" Cindy turned to face Sarah,

"This book, I mean …"

Cindy took the book and pressed it against her, before she smiled at Sarah. "You know, my mother used to believe in the legend of magical books. She always used to tell me that each bookstore has that one mysterious book, meant for one special person. A book so spiritual that it has the power to change one single, heartbreaking event in one person's life. My mother once told me how it could stop time, and give someone one more last chance. Nobody really knows the title of the book, or who the author is, but the story goes that there was once an angel that fell in love with an ordinary man."

She paused to take in a deep breath, before she handed the book back to Sarah.

Sarah gazed down at the leather-bound book, before she looked questioningly up at her mother, "And then, mom?"

"Well, on their wedding day, she confessed her secret to him. She told him that she had fallen from Heaven, just to be with him. She said that she was not of the world, but that her love for him turned her into a human. He was horrified by what she told him, and accused her of being a witch. He left her standing at the altar after he disappeared, never to be seen again. The angel refused to give up on him, and lived out the remainder of her life in solitude while she waited for him. On her death bed, she performed her last powerful deed by adding the unexplained to all bookstores around the world where one book would have the power to take a broken heart back in time, and change the course of the future."

"That is so sad …" She kissed Cindy on the cheek before she quickly made her way into her reading corner.

It was barely an hour later when Sarah heard Simone's welcoming voice, "Hey! Your mom said I'd find you here, what are you reading?"

Sarah closed the book and held it up to Simone. "Passage of Time, it's supposed to be about a legend of time and some fault in the stars …"

"Ooooh, fantasy! I love fantasy!"

"Yeah, I just think, well, I don't really know? But, I think this is the book and that it's all real?" Sarah placed the book down beside her before Simone sat down in front of her.

"What is?"

"Sim, I know this is going to sound weird, but please, please, just keep an open mind?"

"Okay ..."

"Do you think that it's possible to go back in time? I mean, like a do-over?"

Simone frowned, before she burst out laughing. "That is impossible. You'd need a time machine, and one has never been invented."

"Come on, Sim, don't you think there is a kind of magic that makes these things happen?"

"No, I don't, and you, you're supposed to be the smart one, Sè."

Sarah lowered her head, unsure of what to say next. "You're going to be the town's favorite hair dresser and beautician someday, Sim ..." Sarah whispered softly before

Simone burst out laughing again.

"Funny girl! And you, Sarah, what are you going to do?"

"Well, it turns out that I write books, and I live in the city."

"Yeah, right. You will never leave Daniel behind."

"I did, Sim. I just had this idea in my head that I needed to become someone wonderful for him, so I left ..."

"Sarah, you're honestly not making any sense?"

"Sim, please, you have to listen to me. I need someone to believe me. Daniel leaves with his family in December. They are going to sail to Spain for the holidays to spend a last holiday with his grandmother, but Danny, he comes back sick ..." She paused to take in a deep breath.

Simone gazed incredulously at her, as she listened to her best friend tell her about events that have not yet happened.

"Only, no-one knows that he's caught this virus, Sim. It's only in 1997 that he gets sick. And, they can't cure him, and for three years, he suffers while they try everything to save him. But Sim? He eventually dies. In March of 2000, Daniel dies, and no-one tells me until you do when I come home eleven months later!" Sarah was unable to control the tears that had begun to torrent from her eyes.

Simone took her into her arms, and held her firmly against her. She was at once overcome with fear when she heard what Sarah had to say, but more so, when she realized that Sarah believed that it all had in fact, happened.

"Simmy, please, I need you to believe me? I can't tell anyone else and Danny thinks I just dreamed it all." She retreated slightly, before she stared at Simone who was clearly having a hard time believing her. "Sim, I know how this sounds! I know! I wouldn't believe me either, but, I was at his grave yesterday, and today, today I woke up sixteen again? I don't know how to explain it, Simmy, Danny doesn't believe me."

"You told Daniel?"

"I had to. I have to stop him from going to Spain, Sim!"

"Wow Sarah? I mean, it sounds ridiculous, but I know you, and I know that you believe it. Wasn't it just a dream?"

"No, Daniel asked me the same question."

Sarah grabbed the leather-bound book, and handed it to

Simone. "Read this …"   She turned the book over and remained silent as Simone read it.

"For one moment in time, for one call of the heart and the mind to the soul, time is nothing. When the soul agrees that there might have been a fault in the stars, the heart, the mind and the soul will come together, and alter one moment in time."

"Sim, I swear it, I didn't dream it. Daniel is going to die, and there will be nothing any of us can do if he leaves for Spain! You have to help me!"

"How?"

"I don't know? I have to speak to Anabel, and at least, I have to speak to Daniel again …"

"Have you told your mom?"

"No …"

"You should speak to your mom, Sè, she'll believe you, and she'll know what to do? You can't go around saying these things, people will think you're crazy!"

Sarah lowered her head before she took the book from Simone, and hid it on a shelf behind her, just as she had done so many years before.

"So, listen, we're having a get together on the beach tonight. Daniel will be there, will you come? I know that Megan will be coming too?"

"Yeah ..."

"Okay, well I must run, nobody else dies, right?" Simone turned back to face Sarah.

"No ..."

Sarah took her school bag, and quickly made her way back to her mother, who had finished packing the last of the books away. "Sorry, mom. I promise I'll come and help again over the weekend."

"No problem, my girl ..." She turned back to Sarah and took her hands into her own. "Do you want to talk, honey?"

"Maybe later mom ... everyone is getting together on the beach, and I promised Sim I'd go ..."

"Alright, just don't be too late, okay?"

"I won't ..." She placed her arms around her beloved mother, and hugged her tightly. "I love you, mommy ..."

Alice VL

THE BOOKSTORE SERIES
Passage of Time – Book 1

"I love you too, angel …"

When she reached the door of the bookshop, she turned back to Cindy who was staring distraughtly at her. "Mom?"

"Yes?"

"Can I write from the bookstore someday? I mean, can I write my books here and work here, with you?" Cindy walked up to Sarah, and placed her hand on her shoulder, "There is nothing in the world I want more …"

"Thank you, mom …"

"Sarah, what about the dreams you had of moving to the city and becoming someone big, important and wonderful when you were just a little girl?"

"I know mom, but it turns out that my wonderful is right here." She smiled sadly before she hurried back home.

When she walked through the front door of their farmhouse, Megan swiftly ran up to Sarah. "Hey Sè, do you know if David will be there tonight?" David Dawson was a close friend of Daniel. Megan had lost her heart to him in primary school, and was anxious to get him to notice her.

Alice VL

"Yeah, I think so?"

"Oh good!" She screeched as she excitedly clapped her hands.

Before Megan turned away, Sarah grabbed her by her arm, "Megs?"

"Yes?"

"Don't try so hard, sissy, David is going to marry you someday, you know?"

"Yeah, right!" She giggled before she hurriedly made her way upstairs. Sarah followed close behind her, before she ran into Robert.

"Hey Sè, are you feeling better?"

"Why do you ask?"

"Well, this morning? You didn't seem quite like yourself?"

Sarah smiled miserably, before she turned away from him, "I'm fine, thanks, Robbie ..."

When she reached her bedroom, she placed her bag on

the floor, and collapsed onto her bed. She laid staring at the ceiling, reflecting on all that was happening around her. "If this is a dream, why am I not waking up?" She whispered before she turned on her side, and closed her eyes, "If this is magic, why won't anyone believe me? How am I supposed to change anything when no-one will believe me?"

She sobbed softly, before she opened her eyes and stared out in front of her. When she glanced at her wristwatch, she realized that it was a quarter to seven. She had fallen asleep, and when she sat up straight, she knew that she could not sleep in a dream, or dream another dream, in a dream.

She had no idea of what was happening to her, and she was not quite sure that she had wanted to be caught up in a moment, she could never change or alter the course of.

She was flung back into a time where it was expected of her to act sixteen again, when she was living her life as a grown, successful and independent woman only days before.

She was compelled to obey her parents and adhere to their rules, when her heart was that of a much older woman. Sarah realized that she had found herself in a moment in time she was not prepared to recreate, but a moment she had begged for.

She had beseeched the universe for a do-over, and she was given exactly what she had requested and negotiated for. She was given her one more last chance to do all she could, to change and alter a certainty that Daniel would die.

She had her wish and her return to before, to save Daniel, and to ultimately, save her heart. She knew that she could never tell anyone the truth, but that she had her one last chance to do whatever it took, to save his life, and hers.

She slowly made her way to her closet, and quickly pulled out a pair of shorts and a t-shirt. She untied her hair and left it to lay loosely down her back. She quickly grabbed a sweater, and hurriedly made her way downstairs. "Hey dad, have you seen Megs? Has she left yet?" She was in high spirits when she found her father in front of the television, sipping on his whiskey and dragging on his cigar. When she breathed in the aroma of his tobacco, she was once again, thankful to experience the little things that made their house a home while reliving the little things she had forgotten not too long ago.

"She's in the kitchen with mom."

"Thanks, dad."

Alice VL

THE BOOKSTORE SERIES
Passage of Time – Book 1

Sarah made her way into the kitchen, and found Megan and Cindy packing the last of the dishes away.

"There you are, I was about to leave without you." Megan smiled, before she swiftly planted a kiss on Cindy's cheek.

"You girls behave ..."

"Of course, mama, love you."

"Sarah, wait up for just a second?"

"What's wrong, mommy?"

"Nothing. Are you sure you're alright?"

"Yes, I'm fine, I love you, mom." Sarah whispered before she followed Megan out to her car.

Cindy couldn't shake the feeling that something was wide off the mark with Sarah. It felt to her as though her youngest daughter had grown up almost overnight. Her carefree ways and her untroubled days seemed to be a thing of the past. Cindy could almost see the world weighing down heavily on Sarah's shoulders. She could not quite put her finger on it, but she was convinced that all was not well with Sarah.

She anxiously made her way into the living room, and sat

Alice VL

down on the coffee table in front of Thomas. "Is it my imagination, or is something up with Sè?"

Thomas placed his cigar in the ashtray and sat up straight. "You see it too?"

"Yeah, and I mean, she must have told me a hundred times today that she loves me. Robert said the same thing earlier?"

Thomas folded his hands and rested his chin on them.

"She doesn't want to move to the city anymore. She wants to stay here and write from the bookstore?"

Thomas shook his head before he frowned, "Maybe it's just a stage she is going through, have you tried talking to her?"

"Yes, today at the bookstore. She just said she didn't want to talk about it?"

He took Cindy's hands into his, and smiled when he gently squeezed them, "She'll come to you honey, she always does. Just give her time."

"She is scaring me, Thomas. I have never known Sarah to become so withdrawn and sad?"

When they pulled up at the beach, Megan climbed out first, and excitedly made her way onto the beach, to David who was standing around a bonfire they had built only moments before.

Sarah sat in the car for a while longer, before she got out and made her way over to a group of girls that were laughing and chatting while seated on a blanket.

When she reached them, she smiled and quickly greeted the crowd, before she turned to find Daniel. When she saw him standing beside David, she turned around to make her way over to him.

"Wait Sè! Look what I found!" Simone shoved a photograph into Sarah's hand, and giggled softly. It was a picture of Sarah and Daniel when she was a measly four years old, and he barely eight years old. Sarah smiled when she thought back to their childhood, and how she could barely imagine her life without him. "I'm going to show Danny!" Simone grabbed Sarah by her hand and quickly made her way over to Daniel.

"Hey, I'm glad you came …" Daniel placed his arms around her, and held her firmly against him.

When she stepped back, Simone placed the photograph

in Daniel's hand. "Oh man, look at us!" Daniel smiled and looked at Sarah who seemed to grow sadder by the minute.

Before she could reply, Kimberly had made her way over to them. "Oh my, Sarah, you've always been ugly!"

Sarah glared at her, before Simone grabbed the photograph from her hands. Daniel turned to face Sarah, who had turned away from him. He frowned when he noticed her eerie silence, and once again, he was sure that Sarah was not herself. It would have been nothing for Sarah to rip into Kimberly, and entirely tear her apart. Sarah had never backed off from an insult, let alone a fight. Simone glanced over at Daniel when they realized that Sarah had no interest in retaliating against Kimberly's rude insults.

"What's the matter with you, Kim? Always a bitch?" Kimberly grinned when Simone approached her, ready to defend her friend's honor.

Sarah grabbed her from behind, "Come on, Sim, let's go."

Daniel was enraged by Kimberly's behavior, and reprimanded her at once, "Kimberly, I can't believe you just said that!"

"Oh, come on, Daniel. What you see in her, I will never know!"

"You know what, you will never understand that I love her, and I always have, and I can promise you, I always will." Kimberly turned away from Daniel, and nonchalantly made her way over to the group around the bonfire.

When they reached the blanket, Sarah turned to Simone, "I don't really want to be here, Sim. I'm going to go; will you forgive me?"

"Yeah sure, are you okay?"

"Yeah, it's just been such a long day. Tomorrow will be better, I'm sure ..."

As she waved Simone goodbye, Daniel hurriedly caught up with her. "Are you leaving?"

"Yeah ..."

"I'll drive you ..." She smiled when he clutched her hand into his and squeezed it tightly.

When they reached his car, he opened the passenger door for her. Before she climbed in, she turned to face him,

THE BOOKSTORE SERIES

Passage of Time – Book 1

"Danny, let's drive up to the mountain like we used to?"

"Okay, sure, but, we still do it all the time?" Daniel closed the door just as soon as she slid in, and made his way around the driver's seat.

When he turned his car on, he took her hand, and gently kissed it.

They drove up to the mountain in silence. Sarah peered through the car window and couldn't help but notice how beautiful their village lights shone and reflected onto the ocean.

She had missed those moments with Daniel. It felt to her as though she was feeling all the emotions she once fell for him, for the very first time. She was desperate to take in the sounds of the night, and the way he looked at that very moment.

She wanted to look into his eyes and remember the way he looked back at her. She was desperate to plunge into each moment she had with him, and take in all she had once taken for granted.

As they drove up to the spot they would sit and watch the village from, she couldn't understand why she was so desperate to leave Hazel Creek, and swop their beautiful village

Alice VL

for Queenstown. She missed their town. She missed the serenity, and she missed how uncomplicated it all seemed to her.

Alice VL

THE BOOKSTORE SERIES
Passage of Time – Book 1

Alice VL

PART SEVEN

When they reached the mountain, Sarah climbed out of the car, and slowly made her way to a rock she had sat on almost a thousand times before. Daniel sat down beside her, and stared out in front of him. "I left all this behind once, you know?"

Daniel turned to face her, and was once again, totally bewildered and caught off-guard by what she was saying.

"I chose Queenstown over this. I chose the city over you. I was such a fool ..." She lowered her head, when she felt the tears luster in her eyes.

"Sè, I don't know what's going on with you, but you are scaring me. You say things like this, and I don't know what's going on?"

"I know, Danny. I know it's crazy. I know, but just listen to me, okay? You can't not listen to me ..."

He shook his head before he gazed out in front of him,

"I wanted to go and write in the city. I wanted to be the best. I wanted to be someone. I wanted the city lights, the fame and the fortune, and then, then, I wanted to come home to you, and you'd be proud of me. I wanted to matter to the world, Danny, to you, and to the world." She paused to take in a deep breath. "But, I came home too late, Danny. And each time I achieved something wonderful, I wanted more, so, I stayed. I was going to stay for a year, but I ended up staying for twelve. I came home too late." She took his hand into hers and placed her other hand over it. "You didn't tell me. You didn't let anyone else tell me that, that you were sick. I didn't know, Danny?"

"Sarah ..."

"Please Danny, let me talk ..." She got up and knelt in front of him. She took both his hands, and gazed into his bewildered eyes.

"Years from now, Danny, they're going to tell you that you caught a virus, and your parents will figure out that it was this year, this trip planned for December. You are going to suffer so badly, and there isn't a single doctor in the world that can help you, or save you. It's going to attack your heart, and by the time they diagnose your condition, it will be too late for a heart transplant. There will be nothing anyone can do for you; don't you get it?" When her tears began to gush uncontrollably from her eyes, she rested her head on his knees and sobbed wretchedly.

"I don't know what to say, Sarah? I don't know how to respond to this. It's like you're someone else?"

She looked up, and climbed onto his lap, before she took his face into her hands, "I am someone else, Danny. I am older. I have changed. This has changed me. I have been gone for so long, and I wish I never left. I am not the girl I once was. Danny, just say that you believe me. Don't go, please Danny? Don't go, I swear, I won't move to the city. I will stay right here, but swear to me that you won't go?"

Danny felt fear invade his entire being when he noticed the unanticipated desolation in her eyes, and heard the utter desperation in her voice. He slowly wiped the tears that were pouring from her eyes. He had never seen them so sad, and he had never heard such an enormous amount of distress in her voice.

Sarah moved closer until her lips touched his. She closed her eyes, wanting to take in all there was about Daniel Kingsley again. She wanted to feel his lips on hers, and she wanted to breathe in the smell of him again. She wanted to feel his arms around hers. She wanted to feel him again. She wanted to feel something other than numb again. Since finding out about his death, Sarah spent her days in a wandering haze, angry at him, and angry at the world. Her heart had shattered into a thousand pieces, but at that very moment, Daniel's touch was mending what little was left of her.

He kissed her back and pressed her against him. He closed his eyes, and couldn't help but feel a kind of passion he had never known before. His entire body craved hers, while his lips searched hers over and over again.

"Danny ..." She whispered hoarsely before she hurriedly unzipped his jeans. She lifted herself just enough to pull down her shorts before she pressed herself on top of him.

"Sarah?"

"Don't say anything, Danny. Don't say anything. Don't tell me to stop ..."

"You're sixteen, Sè ..."

"I'm not, Danny, I'm not sixteen ..." She let out a faint moan, and when he forcefully pressed her down, she threw back her head, and cried out in exhilaration.

He pulled her against him, before she rested her head on his shoulder. "I love you, Sè …" He whispered breathlessly before she buried her head in his neck.

"I love you, Danny …"

They sat like that for what felt like forever, before Sarah climbed off, and quickly pulled her shorts back up. She sat down beside him on their rock, and gazed out over their village. "Danny, just promise me, promise me you will never leave me? I know you don't believe me, but I need you to promise?"

He turned to face her, and took her face into his hands. "I can never leave you, Sarah Swanson, I'm going to marry you someday …"

She smiled sadly when she realized that if he was to go on that trip, none of what she dreamed of at that very moment would come true. "I will marry you, Daniel Kingsley on the 22nd day of March 2000. Not a day before …"

"You'll be thirty, and I'll be thirty-four?"

"But, you'll be alive, Danny …"

Alice VL

"What do you mean, Sè?"

"You die March, 21st of that year."

Daniel frowned again, and for the first time since she had begun her incoherent talk, he saw something in her eyes that told him, she truly believed it all.

"I don't want to marry you, and then you die, Danny. You only get sick eleven years from now ..."

"Alright Sarah, I will wait for you at the altar in March, on the 22nd day in the year 2000. That makes it fourteen years from now. It's a date Mrs. Kingsley ..."

She smiled dejectedly before she bowed her head, "That's if ..."

"Yeah, let's see." He held her intimately against him, and gently stroked her hair.

When Daniel drove her home, he kept glancing over at her. She was deep in thought while staring at the night lights that were shining all around them. "So, you leave me, huh?"

She turned to face him and nodded, before she smiled sadly. When they reached the ranch, Sarah quickly kissed him on his cheek, before she made her way indoors.

When she reached the front door, she turned around, and was just in time to watch him drive out through the farm gate. She couldn't help but feel that it was all for nothing, and that Daniel would board that ship when the time came. Opening their front door, her tears began to trickle from her eyes once again.

"Sè?" Claire was on her way upstairs when she found Sarah in tears at the front door.

"It's nothing, Claire ..."

"It's not nothing, what's the matter? Mom!" Claire turned around before she shouted into the kitchen.

Cindy hurriedly made her way over to Sarah, and worriedly placed her arms around her. "Come on, my girl, let's go upstairs ..."

Claire stood staring at them, before she made her way upstairs and disappeared into her own bedroom. Sarah collapsed onto her bed, and when Cindy closed her bedroom door, she sat down beside Sarah. "You have to talk to me, baby?"

Sarah sat up and began fidgeting. "It's of no use,

mommy! Nobody believes me! Nobody listens to me!"

"What are you talking about, Sè?"

She turned to face her mother, and from the look in Sarah's eyes, Cindy knew that Sarah was in fact, carrying the burden of the entire world on her shoulders.

"I don't know how to tell you, mom? It sounds so crazy! Daniel thinks so, Sim thinks so, and I can't prove any of it! Nothing I say, I can't prove anything, mommy?" Sarah shouted out through the tears that were spilling from her eyes.

"You can tell me anything, baby girl? Just spill it. Let it come ..."

Sarah lowered her head, and when she folded her hands into each other, she looked up at Cindy one more time. "Yesterday, I came home, mommy. I came home from the city. I live there now, but, I came home to Daniel's grave. Yesterday, was 2001, and I came home eleven months after he died. And then, I fell asleep on his grave, and when I woke up this morning, I was back here. In the now, back in 1986 and I don't know what to do? It was 2001 just yesterday? I was thirty-one years old just yesterday?"

"Sarah, I don't understand? What are you saying?"

Sarah bowed her head one more time, when her bottom lip began to quiver. "I am thirty-one years old, mommy. Megan is a mom. You have two grandchildren, Melissa and Michael. She marries David, and Benjamin is going to build beautiful buildings right here on the ranch. Claire is going to sell houses, and Robert ends up being an amazing doctor, mommy! And Daniel, he, he dies ..."

"Sarah, you're scaring me ..."

She looked up and could barely utter a word over the restriction in her throat. "I know, mommy. I'm scared too. I don't know why I am back here? I don't know what I must do? I first thought I was dreaming, but I'm not waking up? I keep thinking that, that this is my one more last chance? That somehow, God gave me this do-over? I don't think I can live without Daniel?"

She fell into her mother's chest and sobbed fiercely in her mother's arms.

Cindy back-tracked slightly, before she lifted Sarah's chin. "Honey, get some sleep. We'll talk about this again tomorrow, okay?"

"You don't believe me either?"

"That's not what I am saying, Sè. I need to wrap my mind around this, and I want you to get in a good night's sleep, that's all."

Sarah laid her head on her pillow, and turned her back to Cindy. Cindy covered her with a quilt before she turned off the light, and closed the bedroom door behind her. She quickly made her way downstairs, where she found Thomas at the kitchen table.

"Is she okay?"

"Yeah, she's just tired. Is Megan home yet?"

"No, not yet."

"Well, you go to bed, I'll wait up for her."

"Are you sure?"

"Yes, you've had a long day, go to bed."

"Alright, night honey ..." He quickly kissed Cindy on her cheek before he made his way upstairs.

Cindy poured herself a cup of coffee, and sat down at the

kitchen table. She replayed her conversation with Sarah repeatedly in her mind, and each time she heard Sarah tell her that she had crossed the passage of time, Cindy felt her heart hammer as though it was racing at the speed of a freight train.

It felt to her as though she was reliving a moment she had once spent with her own mother, when she was only a little girl. It all felt so familiar to her, and the conversation she had just had with Sarah, was almost identical to a conversation she once had with her mother.

Her heart began to hammer in her chest when she realized that her mother might once have told her the truth, and yet, she had never believed her.

When she heard the front door open, she glanced at her wrist watch, and realized that it was after two the morning. She must have fallen asleep on her arms at the kitchen table, and when Megan walked in, she was surprised to find her mother slightly unsettled at the kitchen table. "Mom, is everything alright?"

"You're late, Megs?"

"I know. Sorry mom. Is Sarah home?"

"Yes, she's upstairs asleep. Sit down, Megan …"

"I'm sorry, mom, it won't happen again …"

"You're right, it won't, but that's not what I want to talk about."

"Okay?"

"Are you still on track to become a teacher?"

"Yes? I start college after I graduate next year, why?"

"Are you going to marry David Dawson someday?"

Megan bowed her head, unable to look her mother in the eye. "I, I don't know? I love him, mom. But, I swear, I will finish college first. Who's been talking to you?"

"Are you going to have children?"

"I guess?"

"What will their names be?"

"What?"

"It's a simple question, Megan, what will their names be?"

"I don't know, mom? I haven't thought that far yet?"

"Come on Megan, long before you or any of your brothers or sisters were born, I had names picked out for you. I chose your names when I was just a little girl."

"Well, I haven't, but I do love Melissa for a girl, and Michael for a boy." Cindy froze when she heard Megan utter the two names Sarah had given her only hours before. Her hands began trembling when she gazed sternly into Megan's eyes, "Have you ever said that to anyone before? Have you told Sarah?"

"No, come on mom! I don't even know if I am going to have children. They are names I like and obviously, David would have a say in it too. So, no, I am not about to go around naming children that I don't even have yet!"

She got up, and stared questioningly at Cindy, "What's all this about?"

"Nothing, go to bed. This conversation does not leave this kitchen, do you understand?"

"Fine." Megan hurriedly made her way upstairs and into her bedroom.

Alice VL

Cindy buried her head in her hands, and thought back to a story her own mother once told her. The story her mom once told her when she was barely seven years old. She hastily made her way upstairs, aware of her own heart pounding ferociously in her chest. She gently opened Sarah's bedroom door, and softly walked over to where her daughter lay sleeping.

She stood staring at Sarah, and was saddened by the fresh tears that laid warmly on her cheeks. She placed her hand on Sarah's shoulder, and gently nudged her, "Sarah? Sarah, wake up."

Sarah turned to find her mother standing at the side of her bed, and at once, she sat up straight. "Mom? What's the matter?"

"Nothing. Here, put this on and come with me …" She handed Sarah her robe, and lifted the quilt off her.

"Where are we going?"

"You'll see …"

They tiptoed down the stairs and out to the front door. Cindy grabbed her car keys, and softly opened the door. When they reached her car, Cindy signaled for Sarah to climb in. They drove out of the ranch in silence, and when they reached the bookstore, Sarah turned to her mother, "The bookstore?"

"Come on …" She switched off the car, and hurriedly unlocked the large, wooden door to the bookstore.

When the both walked in, Cindy closed and locked the door behind them. "Go get that book I gave you …"

Sarah frowned and quickly made her way to her reading lounge. She took the leather covered book, and hurriedly made her way back to Cindy. Cindy took the book from her before she took Sarah's hands, and led her out into the communal reading area.

They sat down on the enormous cushions that lay scattered for their readers, before Cindy hurriedly read the blurb at the back. "Do you know what this means, Sè?"

"No?"

"I got you this book, because it once belonged to my mother. She owned this book, and would never let it out of her sight. She would read to me from it, but she never once allowed me to take it. It took me years to trace it and buy it back. I don't even know why I wanted the book back, but for some reason, it kept haunting me."

Cindy smiled while gently stroking the book. "My mom lost it when we moved, but she believed that this book had a legend of its own, and that this was the book I told you about earlier. The legend of the angel, remember? Her name was Adelaine Alandrali, and some believed she died of a broken heart."

Sarah frowned nervously as she listened to her mother tell her the story of the fallen angel who had died from a broken heart.

"My mother once told me how, how I was struck by a car when I was just a little over five years old. She said that I was killed instantly, and that there was nothing anyone could do to save me. My mom said that she picked up my lifeless body, and refused to hand me over to the coroner. She said that her grief almost killed her too. She told me how she laid on my grave after my funeral, and wished with all her heart to go back in time and save me. She begged God for her one more last chance, just like you did, Sarah. She said that she was sure she would die of a broken heart, just as you are sure you cannot live without Daniel."

Sarah's eyes grew bigger as she attentively listened to her mother, unable to fully understand what she was saying to her.

"She said, she told me that she fell asleep amidst an enormous storm that had unexpectedly escalated around her, and that she was sure she was struck by lightning, but when she woke up, she woke up in her bed on the morning of the day that I was supposed to die."

"Mommy, what are you saying?"

"I don't know, baby? I never believed her, you know? And now you, you come to me with an almost identical story? I must believe you. I have to believe my mother." Cindy took her daughter's hands and brought them to her face. "My mother saved me that day, Sè. Somehow, that book gave her a wish of her mind, her heart and her soul when they were perfectly aligned in one wish, just like it says on the back. She was given the gift of going back to one moment in time, and altering the course and the sequence of unfortunate events that were about to take place. I was just a little girl, so it was as simple as keeping me indoors on that da...."

"Oh mommy ..." Sarah embraced her mother, and held

her tightly against her before she began sobbing once again.

"I spoke to Megan when she came home. Guess what she plans on naming her children someday?"

"Melissa and Michael?"

"You got it!"

Cindy wiped the tears that were beginning to shimmer in her own eyes, and smiled sadly at Sarah. "So, my angel, you do whatever it takes. If Daniel is going to die, you came back because you could save him. You came back, because there was a way to save his life. Whatever it is, you must find it. You must find a way to convince him that all this is going to happen exactly as you say it is. It won't be easy, Sarah, but your one more last chance is now. By the way, you really left us?"

"Yeah, but not this time, mommy. I am going to write beautiful stories right here, from this bookstore. Our magical bookstore! I love you, mommy!"

"I love you too. We must keep this between ourselves, okay? The others won't understand …"

"Okay, mommy …"

Alice VL

"Come on, put that book away, let's go home before anybody notices we're gone."

Sarah quickly hid the book on the shelf in her reading lounge before they made their journey back to the ranch. When they stepped inside, Sarah kissed her mother on her cheek, and tiptoed back upstairs, and into her bedroom.

Cindy stood staring at Sarah for what felt like forever. For the first time that day, it seemed as though a mountain had been lifted off her daughter's shoulder.

When Sarah awoke the following morning, she hurriedly made her way downstairs to find Megan and Claire at the breakfast table. She swiftly glanced around her, before taking an empty seat next to Claire. "Good morning, sisters ..." She smiled when she noticed the confusion in her sisters' eyes.

"Okay? Morning, Sè?" Megan stared at Sarah, unsure of what to say next. Claire shook her head as she sipped on her coffee.

"Good morning, girls!" They all smiled when Cindy stroll in.

"Sarah, how did you sleep?"

Alice VL

"Good, mom. I slept right through …"

"I'm glad, you look much better." Cindy smiled before she handed Sarah a cup of coffee.

"Mom, is Sarah okay?" Megan frowned before she turned to her mother.

"Oh, she's just fine."

Sarah lowered her head, afraid that Megan might see right through her. "Do you want a ride, Sarah?" Claire got up from her seat and grabbed her sling bag.

"No thanks, I am going to walk …"

"Alright then …"

"Can I get a ride with you, Claire?" Megan jumped up and ran after Claire as she made her way out of the front door.

"So, mom, I was thinking … I want to write about this. What is happening now, I want to tell it. And, I was thinking of calling it 'A Moment in Time.' What do you think?"

"I think it's a start. Of course, you could label it as non-fiction if you like?"

"Or based on real events?"

"I'm just worried about, you know? The backlash from the community? I remember how my own mother was labelled a crazy person, and I don't want that for you ..."

"Yeah, you're right, mom. Maybe, maybe Daniel will believe me if he reads it?"

Cindy walked up to her, and placed her arms around Sarah's shoulders. "You have time, my darling. It won't be easy, but you've been given time ..."

Sarah smiled before she placed her coffee mug on the table, and picked up her school bag. "See you after school, mom. I never thought I'd have to relive these awful years again." She burst out laughing before making her way to their front door.

When she opened the front door, Thomas hurriedly made his way indoors. "Daddy, I love you." Sarah held him firmly against her, before she walked out and closed the door behind her. He hurriedly made his way into the kitchen where Cindy was clearing the breakfast table, "I just can't put my finger on it?" He whispered before he sat down at the kitchen table.

"What do you mean?" Cindy placed a cup of coffee in

front of him and frowned.

"That child, Sarah. She's different somehow?" Cindy hurriedly turned away from him, and began packing the dishes away. "She's at that age, just give her time ..." Cindy tried to mask her conversation with Sarah the night before.

"Yeah, I guess. I just can't remember Claire or Megan going through this. Sarah seems so ... old?"

"She's an old soul, Tom, let her be ..."

THE BOOKSTORE SERIES
Passage of Time – Book 1

Sarah knocked softly on Daniel's front door, and when Margie opened it for her, she was desperate to once again, convince her to tell Daniel the truth.

"He's in his room …" Margie turned away from her, before Sarah grabbed her by the arm. "Margie, please, you have to tell Daniel the truth. I know you don't believe me, but he is going to die if you don't …"

"Stop, Sarah! Just stop! There is something seriously wrong with you! I don't know how you know, and I don't know who you've been speaking to, but you are confused and totally out of line!"

"No! If you tell him the truth, he might believe me!"

"You are a crazy person, Sarah! Just stop this nonsense! I don't know what your endgame is, but if you think you can humiliate me, you should think again!" Margie freed her arm from Sarah before she disappeared into her bedroom.

Sarah slowly made her way to Daniel's bedroom, and stood staring at him for what felt like hours. She could barely imagine leaving him, and she could hardly imagine him dying in a few years from that moment.

Alice VL

"Hey Sè …"

Sarah walked in and sat down beside him. She swallowed back on the lump in her throat, desperate to hide the tears that were laying shallow in her eyes.

"Sarah?" Daniel placed his arms around her, and held her firmly against him. She buried her head in his chest, before erupting devastatingly in his arms. "Danny, please don't go …" She dug her nails into his chest when she began sobbing uncontrollably.

"Sarah, I, I know you're upset, but I promise you, you were just dreaming. We've been to Spain a hundred times before, and I'm fine?"

"Danny, this time, you won't be …" She wiped the tears from her eyes, gazing into his, unsure of how to make him understand.

"My grandmother, this will be our last visit, Sè. I have to go."

"I know, Danny. She dies shortly afterwards. You'll never go back, which means this is when you catch the virus. Please, I am begging you, please believe me?"

Alice VL

"I believe you are afraid, Sarah. But, you cannot predict the future, nobody can. Nobody knows what will happen tomorrow?"

"I do. I know, Danny. I don't know how it happened, but one moment I was at your grave, and the next, I am here again. I have this one chance, Danny, and you are taking it away from me! I get this one do-over, and you won't believe me! I don't know how to do this alone? I don't know what to say to make you believe me? I don't know what to do? You are going to die, Daniel! Megan is going to marry David. I am going to leave you, and never see you again! Simone opens up a hair and beauty salon and your sister, Daniel, she plans weddings! She displays little miniature wedding cakes! And she's angry! And she's old! And she blames me! And I, Danny, I will die, and everyone will think it's the storm, but it won't be. It will be from a broken heart on your grave because I, I can't live without you! Even though I leave you for so long, I can't live without you."

"Stop saying that, Sarah ..." Daniel got up and swiftly pulled on a jacket. "Let's go, you're going to be late for school."

Sarah took her bag and when she looked at Daniel one more time, she realized that he would never believe her. There was nothing more she could say, to make him believe her.

Alice VL

When he pulled up at school, he felt immense guilt for snapping at her only moments before, yet, he couldn't discard her haunting performance or the words she viciously spewed at him. He felt fear consume his entire being when he considered for a single moment that Sarah was not imagining any of what was to come, in the not too distant future. "Sè, do you want to do anything tonight? We haven't been out for a movie in ages?"

Sarah looked over at him, and felt entirely defeated and wholly conquered, "I am going to the bookstore after school. If you like, you can join me there tonight. I want to show you something, I want to try and explain …"

"Sounds good. I'll bring pizza."

She kissed him on his cheek before she opened the door, and made her way over to where Simone was standing. Daniel waved when she turned back, and could not shake the feeling that Sarah had become distant and sad.

Alice VL

When Sarah arrived at the bookstore after school, she was relieved to find Cindy organizing new books that were delivered that morning. "Hi mom!"

"Hello my darling, I'm glad you came. We have some wonderful new books that I think you might enjoy." Cindy smiled and was excited to show Sarah the new stock. Sarah walked up to Cindy, and quickly looked through the books her mother was about to shelve.

"Mommy, I have tried so hard to warn Daniel. I don't know what else to do?"

Cindy placed the books back on the trolley, and turned back to Sarah, "You must keep trying, Sarah."

"I know. I want to stay tonight after you leave. I've invited Daniel over. I want to show him the book, and try one more time. Will that be okay, mom?"

"It's a school night ... I forget you're not sixteen anymore, my girl. Of course, you can. Now come on and help me shelve these books!" Cindy handed a weary Sarah half the stack, and in silence, they continued shelving the new books.

"One of these days, I am going to want to know what

Alice VL

we're like? Do I age gracefully? Is dad as handsome as now? What do Melissa and Michael look like? I have so many questions!" She giggled softly while shelving her new books, one by one.

"I don't know, mommy? I am so ashamed. I don't come home until after Danny dies. You send me photographs, but it's not the same, you know?"

It was just after six that evening when Cindy called out to Sarah who had spent most of the afternoon on her manuscript in her reading room, "I'm leaving honey! Don't forget to lock up when you come home, alright?"

"I won't mom!" Sarah heard the sound of the ever-familiar bell when her mother left through the large, wooden doors of Fine Books.

She had barely focused her attention back to her manuscript, when the same bell warned her that someone had entered. Sarah closed her laptop, and rushed downstairs. She was surprisingly excited to find Daniel standing there, holding the pizza in his hands.

"Come on up, Danny, mom has left …" She smiled before she turned, and led the way upstairs. She took the book from her shelf and sat down on the cushions she placed on the floor.

Alice VL

Daniel sat down beside her, and frowned when he noticed the uncertainty in her eyes. He placed the pizza on a table behind him, before he placed his hand on her knee. "You okay?"

She was gazing at the book in her hands, unsure of how to tell Daniel about 'The Passage of Time,' and how it had magically brought her back to a time she had once forgotten, yet, it was a time that the book had brought her back to, and she had to believe that it was a time that had significant meaning, and that she would understand it someday.

Without looking back at Daniel, she smiled dejectedly, and almost at once, her hands began to quiver.

"Sarah?"

Sarah gently stroked the book before she turned it over. "It says here that for one moment in time, for one call of the heart and the mind to the soul, time is nothing. When the soul agrees that there might have been a fault in the stars, the heart, the mind and the soul will come together, and alter one moment in time. Do you know what that means, Danny?" She whispered hoarsely before she placed the book down beside her and turned to look Daniel squarely in the eye.

"I guess? I mean …"

Alice VL

"Danny ..." Sarah interrupted, afraid that he might not quite understand. "It means that when your heart, mind and soul has come together after experiencing a devastating event, there is a magic in the pages of this book to take you back in time, and give you one more last chance. Like a do-over ..."

He shook his head, before he interrupted her, "Sarah, again? Magic in a book? This is ridiculous!"

"Danny, it's not. It's happening! Please, Danny, please!" She reached over to him, and climbed onto his lap before she took his face in her hands.

"Sarah, I know you come from a world of books and fairytales and magic ..."

"Danny, just close your eyes and listen to my heart. Feel it, feel my soul ..." She closed his eyes before she gently kissed him on his lips. "Not too long ago, I was wandering around a city street. I had just turned thirty-one, and had never felt more alone in my life than at that very moment. The bright lights, the city nights, the glamour, the fame, the interviews, the fans, none of that mattered to me anymore. It was eleven months ago when I saw an artist painting the most beautiful painting, and I asked him to paint me a love story. You, you told me a few years earlier that you've, you've forgotten me, so I so desperately wanted a new love story, you know?"

Sarah paused to take in a deep breath when Daniel suddenly opened his eyes. "Sè?" He whispered nervously when a shudder entered and overwhelmed his entire body.

She placed her finger on his lips, before she closed his eyes again, "He painted me a love story, Danny, and in it was you, older and greyer, but you. You were always in the stars for me, Danny, and when, when I came home twelve years later, you were gone. I only now put it together that he painted me my love story on the very day that you died. I was too late ..."

Daniel opened his eyes, still entirely dominated by a shudder that had begun crippling him. He gazed into her shimmering eyes and knew at that very moment, that Sarah was hiding a lifetime of sorrow that was glistening through her tears.

"Don't say anything, Danny. I don't want you to say anything. I am asking you to see the signs, and to remember this. Remember me, and when you leave on that ship to Spain, I will make plans to leave for the city as soon as I can. I can't stay here knowing what I know. Maybe, maybe this is how it was meant to be all along. Maybe, I could never change anything. Perhaps, I was never meant to alter any course, but if you, Danny, if you believe me, even just a little, look for the signs, and stay …"

She gently touched his mouth with hers, and firmly pressed herself against him. When a lost tear rolled down her cheek, she held onto him almost as though her life depended on it. She retreated slightly, before she unzipped his jeans.

Daniel turned her around and lay her down on the carpet. He gazed into her eyes, and for a moment, he was sure he could see the exhaustion and defeat in her eyes. He kissed her as though he believed that he would be gone from her soon, and when his hands trailed down her body, she closed her eyes, determined to take in all she could about Daniel Kingsley.

She wanted to remember the way his skin felt on hers, and she wanted to absorb each emotion she felt when he touched her. Daniel closed his eyes, and kissed her gently, "I love you, Sè …" He whispered croakily as his mouth explored every inch of her.

Sarah felt her body come alive as he discovered parts of her, she never thought could send shudders down her spine. Her heart had released itself from the intense pain and anguish it had almost gotten used to, and her mind had shut itself off from the outside world.

She wanted to feel him, breathe him, and explore the parts of her body that had woken up as though it had remained in a deep sleep for a hundred years. When she began to moan softly, Daniel opened his eyes, and gazed at her.

Her eyes were closed, her body had begun to quiver, and her hands were clutching at the carpet underneath her. He looked at her for a moment longer, and was sure that Sarah seemed older than the sixteen-year-old she was.

His heart ached at the thought that she might be telling the truth, but when she opened her eyes and pulled him closer to her, he knew that nothing else mattered at that very moment.

"Sè?"

"Don't say anything ..." She lifted her body until she could feel him, before she gently guided him to her. He moved slowly, while he held her forcefully against him. She tilted her head back, and cried out in animation when her entire body began to shudder uncontrollably.

Daniel watched her as she let out an exasperating moan, and when she looked back at him, he could no longer hold back.

Alice VL

His entire body began to contract in pleasure, and when she placed her arms around him and held him firmly against her, he buried his head in the pillow below her.

He laid holding onto her, gasping for breath. She closed her eyes again, and absorbed one more time how his body felt against hers. It was a feeling Sarah did not want to lose. It was as though he was an extension of her, and his body against hers, felt like home to her.

When he rolled over onto his side, he laid looking at her for what felt like forever. She laid quietly, staring at him as though she might never see him again. When he smiled at her, Sarah knew that her fight was not yet over, and that she would do all she could to convince Daniel that she was not crazy, and that she came back to save him.

To save her. She wanted her love story, and she wanted Daniel. Her heart started hammering profusely when she closed her eyes and saw his grave stone that was burned in her mind, come back to haunt her.

It was real. It happened, and she knew at that very moment that she would not survive losing him. She turned back to Daniel, and gently stroked his cheek, "Danny, I just, I love you so much. I made so many mistakes. I thought we had time. I thought I could find my place in the world when, when it was never really anywhere, but here with you. I was gone for so long, and it was muck later than I thought it was."

Daniel rolled onto his back, and stared at the ceiling without uttering a word. She leaned over to him, and gazed into his frosty eyes, "I know this is a lot. I know I have no proof. I know, Danny, but please, just look out for the signs. Promise me, Danny?"

Daniel took her into his arms, and buried her head in his chest, "I swear, Sè, if that's what you need from me, I can do that. I can lookout for the signs ..." She squeezed him tightly, before she lifted her head, "Daniel Kingsley, I cannot live one single day without you."

"You won't have to ..."

Alice VL

PART EIGHT

Sarah spent every free moment writing her book, 'A Moment in Time' from her mother's bookstore, and late into the night when she was in bed after the entire world around her became silent.

She told the story of the love she had for Daniel, and how foolish she was to leave their little home town, and shoot for the moon while she hoped to land amongst the stars.

She wrote of how she thought of him each day, and how she wanted to give up her life in the city and come home to him on so many, lonely nights.

She told of how she did not quite find what she was looking for, and that she stayed one more year, each year, in the hopes that she could capture her dreams, and bring them with her when she finally came home to him. She wrote of how she longed for her parents, her brothers and sisters, and how her heart ached for Daniel each time she would call him, and hear his voice.

Alice VL

She said how distant she felt as time went by, and how she was sure she no longer belonged in Hazel Creek. She wrote of how she avoided her family, and how her heart would shatter when life in Hazel Creek continued as though she was never a part of it.

She told of the letters she wrote to Daniel that she kept hidden in a drawer, in the corner of her bedroom. She said how wonderful her stories were, and how she could get lost in the worlds of her characters, and how they eventually became family to her.

She wrote of her escape to the universes she had created, and how submerged she became with each new book she would write. She told of the loneliness that entirely overpowered her some nights, but that when she closed her eyes, she could escape into the worlds she wrote about.

She spoke of the men that would wander casually onto her path, and how desperate she was to live as a recluse, when her heart reminded her of her promise to Daniel.

She told of the artist who painted her a love story, and how her soul had nudged her to come home to Daniel. She wrote of the grave she came home to and the words carved in stone, that would haunt her for the remainder of her life.

She said that her heart had shattered into a thousand fragments when she collapsed on his grave. She spoke of the storm that had entirely engulfed her, and how the thunder, lightning and rain and overpowered her. She wrote about waking up in her old bedroom, and how she became sixteen again.

She wrote of The Passage of Time, and how the magic in those pages had once saved her own mother. She told the story of the fallen angel who fell in love before she ultimately lost him, and never saw him again.

Sarah wrote about Daniel, and how daunting he found her story. She wrote about Margie, and how she begged her to tell Daniel the truth. Sarah wrote about their night in the bookstore, and how it would eventually be all she would ever have left of Daniel.

She said that her heart could not predict an ending, and she prayed that Daniel would see the signs, and alter the fate that awaited him once he boarded The Alicia and left for Spain.

She said that there was no ending to write about, and she prayed that Daniel Kingsley would write the final chapter of A Moment in Time.

Alice VL

On each occasion that Sarah ran into Margie, she would once again beseech her to tell Daniel the truth. Margie grew increasingly frustrated with Sarah, and eventually, she completely avoided her.

Sarah would often collapse in Cindy's arms through sheer frustration that she could not get through to Margie, but Cindy would persistently encourage her to try again. For Sarah, it was of no use.

Margie was immensely afraid of her father's reaction, and she feared Anabel's disappointment. Sarah knew that she was fighting a losing battle, but it was all proof she had to convince Daniel that she was telling the truth.

She had lived in another time, one he was no longer a fragment of.

Alice VL

PART NINE

On the morning of December 17th, 1986, Sarah slowly made her way over to the house she would stop by each morning before she left for school, only it was the morning they were to set sail for Spain.

She clutched anxiously onto her manuscript, A Moment in Time, before she began trembling nervously. She stopped, and stood quietly in the shade of an almost fifty-year-old oak tree, from where she eyed the old white house on the hill.

She felt a gentle breeze submerge her, before a mild shudder ran down her spine, almost as though it was welcoming her back, but at the same time, scolding her for being gone for far too long. Almost as though it knew she had been gone, in a whole other time and a whole other life.

She could have sworn that the old oak was much smaller when she used to stand at that very same spot and call out his name, not too long ago.

Alice VL

She could clearly remember how they carved their initials in that very same tree, and when she looked closely, she could see traces of what was once written, and promised in the bark.

Her eyes followed the trail that led up the stairs, and onto the porch that wrapped itself around the entire house. He would someday, not be home, but she would return one last time.

She would come back and ask for her soul to be returned to her. Sarah was ready to plead, beg and negotiate with the house to free her soul now, before Daniel leaves, so she opened the gate and walked up the path she had walked a million times before.

She looked down at her feet and wondered if her footprints were perhaps burned in somewhere underneath her, below a thousand others that would someday, walk the same pathway after her. She wondered if the walls would remember her, and if the rose shrubs would still recognize her when she returned, years from that day?

She beamed slightly when she saw the age-old garden swing, one she could barely remember not being there. Was she seven, or was she nine when she sat there with him, for the very first time? Before she sat down, she gently pressed her hands down on the scuffed and worn swing it would someday become. She couldn't help but wonder if her hand prints would still be hidden beneath his.

The front door was closed, the windows were shut, and the curtains were all drawn. Almost as though it was defending and preserving the memories that would soon be gone, and almost forgotten. Almost as though it was shielding outsiders from the sacredness of a kind of love, that would soon, no longer live there.

Her eyes caught the upstairs window to the bedroom right at the end of the hall. How often had she strolled down that passage and into that bedroom where he would be playing the guitar or waiting for her to stop by before school. She wondered if those four walls ever whispered their stories to anyone else?

Stories they were dreaming of when she was sixteen, seventeen and eighteen. How many secrets had they branded into the walls of that very same bedroom? She looked over at the Fraser Fir she was sure seemed bigger when she was younger.

Was that where her love for Christmas trees and their

magic began? She frowned just a little when she remembered how his beloved dog was buried right below that beautiful tree, and how they both thought that he would live on in that very same tree, forever.

It was so long ago, and yet, it was just the other day. She looked out over the town below the big, white house on the hill, and at once recognized the farm road they had walked each day, hand in hand. She lowered her head, and replayed memories of what felt like a thousand years and a million heartbeats ago.

She reminded herself that she was no longer looking through the eyes of a sixteen-year-old teenager, but through those of a woman who had lived all this once before.

She slowly made her way to the front door, and she wondered how many times she had knocked on that very same door? She was sure that if she listened closely, she might hear the sounds on the other side echo down the hallway, just as she had so many times before. She placed her ear against that heavy, wooden door when she was sure she could hear his laughter on the other side.

She closed her eyes when she heard the ghosts of her past still run wild on the other side of those walls. She could not ignore the sounds her haunting memories of unspoiled and untainted love made, or the promises of forever she could still hear from the house where he would once have lived.

As she made her way down the path and back to the gate, she quickly swabbed at the tears that were threatening to gush from her eyes. It would be her last visit to the house. It would be one final struggle to free her heart, still coldly imprisoned between those walls and under that roof.

It would be her one last chance to walk away, without leaving her soul behind. There, where it continued to dwell in a home that would no longer whisper his name.

When she turned back and reached the gate, she turned around one last time. She whispered a silent goodbye to what was left of the house where her soul would be trapped in forever. A house that would soon, no longer have any stories to tell, except for the collection of souls it would someday, refuse to set free.

A home that would grow cold, abandoned and silenced. The memories of love, laughter and joy that once roamed freely in each room of this home, would soon be carved into the foundation and forsaken. In a few years from that very moment, nobody would want the house where he once lived.

Nobody would want to be reminded of the sorrow or the anguish that came in as an uninvited guest and left a path of destruction on its way out. As though it will stand on sacred ground, the house would be left untouched, in a few short years from that day. Nobody would dare to walk through that gate anymore.

Nobody would willingly want to walk up the trail to the house where Daniel once lived. Nobody would ever forget the anguish of the broken hearts that were left behind, and nobody would be able to fix the fragmented wreck that was once a house where love lived.

The skies turned dark, and the wind howled through the large oak tree as she waved the house goodbye, one last time.

"Sarah!"

She was at once brought back to reality when she heard Daniel call out behind her as she hurriedly headed up the road, and back to her house.

"Sarah! Wait!"

She walked faster, as she hurriedly swabbed at the tears

that were rolling mercilessly from her eyes. She heard him come closer, and stopped, desperate to swallow back on the lump that had begun restricting her throat.

He grabbed her hand, and turned her around to face him, "Sarah?"

She looked up, and when Daniel looked into her eyes, he noticed how red and swollen they were.

"Danny …" She shoved the manuscript in his hands, and hurriedly wiped the tears from her eyes, "I don't know how this story ends? I don't want it, if it ends the way it did once …"

"What story?"

"I started writing this book when I came back in June. I already know how it ended once, Danny, and I, I can't do it again. I can't go through this again. I am hoping, I am so hoping that you read this book, and that you find something in there to tell you that I am not imagining any of this, Danny."

"Sarah?"

"I am begging you, Daniel. Please, please don't board that ship today. Don't board The Alicia …"

Alice VL

Daniel placed his arms around her, and pressed her head against his chest. "Sarah? The Alicia? How did you know?"

"I don't know anymore how to tell you, Danny so no, I can't do this. I have done everything I can to make you stay. I have tried for months to tell you and to make you understand. Margie won't tell you the truth, and you don't believe me. Turn around, and look at your house ..."

Daniel turned back and fixed a gaze on the home he had lived in for all his life. "Years from now, Danny, it will be abandoned. Nobody will want to live here. Nobody will want to come back here. It will be a reminder of how you suffered, and how you died right here, in this house. It will destroy your parents, and it will tear them apart. Margie will grow up to be so angry someday, and Mark, well, I don't know about Mark? But this house, Danny, this house will imprison us forever. All of us."

"Sarah, do you know how you sound when you say these things?"

"Yes Danny, I do know, and I don't care. I don't care that you think I am insane. I don't care how I sound. I have been listening to you tell me for months that I sound like a crazy person. Because you see, I would sound like an idiot any day, if it meant that it would save your life."

"I'll be back so soon, Sarah, and you'll see, nothing will be wrong."

"Yes, Danny, you will be back. And nothing will be wrong for the next eleven years. I don't know how the next eleven years will be, because I won't be here. I have changed. I have lived all of this, once before. I can alter my course and change the path I take. I can stay here in Hazel Creek, and never leave for the city, because I have lived this all once before. I have learnt from this. But what I can't do, Danny, is change yours. Only you can, and you, you just won't listen to me. What I can't do is stay here in Hazel Creek and watch you die a little each day, from the moment you get back."

He took her hands into his, and firmly squeezed them. "Nobody knows, Sè ..."

"You are wrong, Danny, I do. I know. And I can't be with you only to lose you, you know?"

"You're not going to lose me, Sarah ..."

She lowered her head, and freed her hands from his grip, "It's over, Danny. I am leaving. I am going to the city as soon as I can. I want to be gone from here before you get back. This time, Danny, it's me asking you not to call me, and not to make contact with me. I can't go through this again. Perhaps, this is how things were meant to be in the first place. Maybe Danny, maybe, we're not supposed to change anything."

She took his face into her hands, "Maybe, I was never supposed to alter anything ..."

He placed his hands over hers, and frowned when he saw the raw expression in her eyes, "You're leaving Hazel Creek?"

"As soon as I can. I can't watch you die ..."

"We all die, Sarah! From the moment we are born, we begin to die! You can't leave because of a hunch, or a dream, or a vision, or whatever you want to call it?" He raised his voice, before he turned away from her.

She walked up to him, and with his back turned to her, she placed her arms around him, "I can, Danny. I have lived a whole other life. It was not a dream, it was not my imagination. It was real. When I left the first time, I never knew, but now, now I know. This time, you can't hide that you're dying from me and yet, Danny, at this very moment, I wish I never knew ..." She whispered in his ear, as her tears began to bucket from her eyes once again.

He lowered his head, and glanced down at the manuscript in his hands, "Will you come say goodbye at the harbor?"

She moved away from him, and hurriedly swabbed at the warm tears on her cheeks, "Yeah …" She turned away, and quickly made her way back to the ranch next door.

Alice VL

When Sarah strutted in through the front door of the ranch she had found safety, security and comfort in, she collapsed to her knees and cried out in anguish while her tears bucketed unreservedly from her eyes. Cindy found her in the entrance hall, and knelt in front of her, before she placed her arms around her daughter.

"It's too late, mommy ..." She cried out as she clung to her mother. Her heart was hammering so fiercely in her chest, yet at the same time, she could feel it splintering into a million pieces.

"Baby, sometimes, you must just have faith in the knowing that you did all you can do ..."

"Why did I come back then? Why am I here, now? Why have I lived six months here, without being able to change one single thing? I don't understand mommy!" Sarah yelled out as her tears began drowning out her face.

Cindy was frantic to wipe away them away, and for the first time in her life, there was nothing she could say to Sarah to mend the shards of her broken heart.

Sarah whimpered desolately in her mother's arms as they sat on the floor in the entrance hall in silence. When Sarah retreated slightly, she was overcome with devastation, "I know I'm supposed to be sixteen, mom, and I know I have two years left here, but, I have to leave here. I have to get so far away from here as I can. I can't stay, mommy ..."

"Sè? Whether or not you're sixteen, you are trapped in the body of a sixteen-year-old. I can't let you go?"

"Send me to a boarding school, mom, just send me far away from here. I don't ever want to come back. I never want to come back here again. I never want to see Daniel after today again!"

Cindy once again placed her arms around her daughter, and as though her own heart had begun shattering, she realized that she could not go against her daughter's wishes.

Cindy was crushed and utterly wrecked by the mere notion of sending Sarah away, but at the same time, she could in no way at all, bear witness to the hurt and anguish her daughter was feeling at that very moment. There was no way at all that she could witness the pain her daughter would be compelled to endure in the years to come.

She only hoped, and bitterly prayed that the time apart, and before Daniel's impending death, will help her adjust and mend her splintered heart. "Alright, my girl …"

"Thank you, mommy, and dad can never know. Nobody can ever know."

"Come on, go dry those tears, it's almost time to meet the Kingsleys at the dock. Pull yourself together, my girl, and remember, I love you so much …"

"I love you too, mommy. And, I'll never forget this, here, today …"

Alice VL

PART TEN

Sarah held possessively onto Cindy's hand as The Alicia left the dock of the quaint little harbor in Hazel Creek. She felt numb inside, and although that ever-presumptuous lump in her throat had continuously threatened to silence her for the second time that day, there was not a single tear that spilled from her eyes as she watched The Alicia hold Daniel captive, and leave the safe harbor of Hazel Creek.

Sarah knew that when he returned, he would bring with him a shattering plague that would slowly fester inside of him, and rear its ugly head during what was meant to be, the very best years of his life.

It would inhumanely incapacitate him. It would heartlessly claw at him for three long years, while he suffered through debilitating pain and anguish. It would ravage his heart, the one part of him that loved her unconditionally. It would dismantle his family, and destroy their once functional home. Sarah knew from the very essence of her that Daniel would

Alice VL

return, bringing a lifetime of sorrow with him. Her heart had not yet caught up with her fears, and her soul had not yet absorbed a reality of having to lose Daniel all over again.

She gazed over at Daniel who was standing on the edge of the ship looking back at her, until she could barely see him. She waved a final goodbye to the only boy she had ever loved, and she reminded herself to return on the 22nd day of March in the year 2000. The day after he was destined to take his last breath, the day he swore to make her his wife someday.

Daniel and the rest of the Kingsley family waved cheerfully at the Swansons as they set sail for their final holiday in Spain. He tightened his grip onto the manuscript she had given him, and couldn't help but wonder for a moment, if there was perhaps, any truth to Sarah's inexplicable fears.

"What you got there, Dan?" Margie glanced over at the neatly typed out pages in Daniel's hands.

"I, it's Sarah's book, she says she doesn't have an ending for it and wants me to read it."

"Oh?"

"She ... she is so sure that ..."

Alice VL

Margie frowned when she detected the sudden exhaustion and indisputable fear in his eyes. "What Danny?"

"She's leaving for Queenstown. She thinks I'm going to die."

"She thinks you're going to pick up a virus on this trip, I know. I've been listening to her for months! She is deluded and quite a piece of work!"

"Yeah. Wait, what?"

Margie was mortified that she had said it out loud, and instinctively, she bowed her head, unsure of what to say next.

"Margie? What aren't you telling me? Sarah told you? You know?"

"Yeah, she, she kept saying that I could save you if I tell you the truth ..."

"The truth? What are you talking about, Margie?"

She turned away from him, before Daniel forcefully grabbed her by her arm, "What do you know?"

"Danny, I honestly don't believe all that mumble jumble, and you can't tell me that you do either. But ..."

Daniel squeezed her arm tighter, as his heart began thumping profusely. As his breaths grew shorter, Daniel was convinced that someone had reached into his chest and began squeezing his lungs mercilessly. "But?"

"She's right! I have dreamed of becoming an event planner all my life! I want to plan weddings and parties! I don't want to teach children. I don't like kids! I can't stand them! You just, you just can't tell dad! Danny, you cannot tell dad! Not yet and not until I graduate, okay?"

Daniel let go of her arm and stepped back as he tried to take in all that Margie had just confessed to. He was at once overcome by a horrendous, eerie quiver that managed to rip through into the very core of him. "What?"

"Don't tell me that you believe her, Danny?"

Daniel stood staring at her in utter disbelief. He thought back to all the months that Sarah had tried to warn him. He thought about how she begged him to stay behind in Hazel Creek, and not board that ship. She harassed him endlessly, as though her life depended on it.

As he stood there mulling over her words and her endless nagging, Daniel shockingly realized that her story had never changed. Not once did she divert from her story or what she knew to be true all along.

Not for one moment did she alter or amend any fact about her story, and when he paged through to the last typed page of her manuscript, he at once identified the final scene she had written. A scene they had lived only moments before. A scene wherein she was waving him goodbye, for one last time, only it was date stamped and written in August. She couldn't have known.

He gazed up into the sky, and noticed that the clouds had entirely covered up the sun. They had turned into a ghostly and shadowy darkness, and the thunder that had begun to wreak havoc on the clouds, had sent bolts of lightning that began to crash down all around them.

He looked back over at the docks and saw how the rain had come crashing down on her as she stood watching him sail away from her. Yet, as he stood staring at the girl he had said goodbye to only moments before, he was devastated by the image before him.

She was not the young girl he had placed his arms around, only minutes ago. She was older. She looked vulnerable and fragile, and she appeared defeated and exhausted.

He stared at her and realized that he was looking at a woman so much older than the teenager he was leaving behind, one who had lived a hundred years and one who had fought a million fears, cried a thousand tears, and lived a shattered life. He grabbed onto the rails, and at once realized that Sarah was telling the truth all along, and that she had found a way to come back to him. He was seeing the signs she begged him to pay attention to.

She had found a way to trick time into sending her back to that very moment, a moment she had lived once before. He glanced down at her manuscript, and suddenly, it all made sense to him.

She had travelled through the passage of time, frantic to alter her course, and manipulate the cruel twists fate once had in store for them. She came back for her one more last chance, and yet, he was about to steal it from her. He fell to his knees, and while he clutched desperately to her manuscript, he yelled out in anguish, "I have to be where she is, I want my one more last chance."

Alice VL

THE STARS ALL AGREED

"Sarah …" Cindy whispered softly at Sarah, who peeked over her covers, as she gently rubbed her sleepy eyes. "Wake up, honey …" She placed a breakfast tray on her nightstand, and sat down on the bed beside Sarah.

"Breakfast in bed? What's the occasion?" Sarah sat up straight and folded the covers around her, before she let out a nervous giggle.

Cindy frowned slightly before she leaned forward, and gently cleared her unruly hair from her eyes. "It's your wedding day, my darling. The day you've been waiting for, for so long …"

Sarah gazed at her mother as she tried to find evidence in her eyes to tell her that she was teasing her, and for a moment, she wondered whether she was dreaming. She smiled uneasily, and sullenly glared at her before she glanced around her with a sense of urgency as her heart began to thrash violently in her chest. "Very funny, mother!"

Alice VL

Her eyes wandered tensely over to the closet in her old bedroom on the ranch, before she spotted a wedding gown trailing down onto the carpet. She grabbed Cindy's hands when the blood began to drain from her face, as fear began to take a hold of and seize her heart.

"You're getting married today, Sarah …"

Sarah was speechless when she gazed into her mother's eyes. She was at once wholly bewildered and unhinged by her mother's unexpected announcement. Only a day before, did she say goodbye to Daniel as he boarded The Alicia to set sail to Spain.

Only hours ago, did she cry herself to sleep when she failed to convince Daniel to avoid taking that dreaded trip, but to rather, stay behind with her in Hazel Creek. To turn his back on all his doubts, and all his reservations, and to trust her.

It was only yesterday, that she walked away from him, and harshly reprimanded herself for her distinct failure in making Daniel understand that she had returned to a moment in time the universe was sure, she was equipped to alter their course, and the sequence of events that would now, inevitable take place. "Where am I? Mommy? I, I don't understand? I'm getting married? I mean, just yesterday, we said goodbye to the Kingsleys? I am getting married? Today? Who am I getting married to?"

Cindy glowered slightly in skepticism, before she squeezed her daughter's sudden frosty hands. "Honey? What are you talking about? That was fourteen years ago?"

"What? No, no. That can't be. I remember everything? I, it was yesterday?" Sarah at once glanced around her again. She could in no way at all, discard the confusion and disorientation that had begun to overwhelm her.

"What is the date?"

"Oh Lord, don't tell me it's happening again? It's March, the 22nd, 2000. It's the date you chose when you were sixteen. It's March, honey ..."

"Daniel? I am marrying Daniel? He's here? We are in the year 2000? He is alive? He's not sick?"

"Oh honey, of course you're marrying Daniel, and no, he's not sick. He never got sick. They never went on that trip. They never even left the harbor. Don't you remember anything?"

Sarah frowned again but could barely deny the joy that

had suddenly crept up inside of her. "He didn't? They didn't? They never went to Spain?"

Cindy lovingly embraced her as she stroked her daughter's still defiant hair.

"Mommy, I swear, it was only yesterday that we said goodbye to them. I was sixteen only yesterday. I missed this. All of this, I've missed all of this. How? What made them stay?"

"Oh baby, as they were about to leave the harbor, Margie finally confessed and told Daniel about her plans to become an event planner someday. Daniel said that when he turned to the last page of your manuscript, you had written your goodbye to him at the docks, exactly in the way it played out, except that you had written in back in August, and you couldn't have known unless you were there once before. He said, he said that when he looked at you standing on the docks, he saw you, but that you were different. You were much older, and that was when he knew, it was right then that he knew, you were telling the truth all those months. They turned the ship around after Daniel threatened to jump overboard. They never went to Spain, honey, you did it! You saved him!"

Sarah burst out crying before she flung her arms around

her mother, and yielded freely to the tears that were cascading from her eyes. As she held her mother in her arms, she glanced down beside her, and caught a glimpse of a book that was lying on her bed. "A Moment in Time? Is this my book?"

Cindy backed away slightly from Sarah and picked the book up. "It sure is, your very first novel. Do you really not remember any of this?"

"No? I published A Moment in Time? How does it end?" She grabbed the book from her mother's hands, and hurriedly paged through until she reached the very last page. She smiled broadly while reading through the tears that had begun to glisten in her eyes once more. "We have a life. Daniel has life. I never went to the city. I work with you in the bookstore. I write there?"

"You sure do. Just like you said you would. And you've written many, many fine books since this one ..."

"Oh mommy. This was my dream all along. The city was never worth it. The city was my biggest mistake. This is where I belong, here, with Daniel." She flung her arms around her mother one more time, before she hurriedly wiped the tears from her cheeks. She at once thought of Megan, Clare and her brothers. When she took her mother's hand, she felt excitement well up inside of her.

"Don't tell me? Megan and David are married. They have children, Michael and Melissa?"

"They sure do, and let me tell you, they just adore their Aunt Sarah. You are so good with them, Sè, and you've loved them since the moment they were born, as your very own. You spoil them rotten, baby, and you and Megan regularly argue about that."

Sarah erupted into an uncontrollable laughter, and was at once deeply thankful that she hadn't missed out on one single moment with her niece and nephew.

"And Claire? She is one ruthless, bitchy realtor?"

"Right again! Oh Lord, Sè, getting her home, or even to attend family gatherings is a nightmare!"

"And Robert, mom? Robert is one hell of a doctor and Benjamin builds things here on the ranch?"

Cindy burst out laughing, "Ben has actually been building the pergola under which you will be saying your vows today."

Sarah leaped from her bed and rushed over to her

wedding gown. "I have no idea what this looks like? Is it pretty, mom?" She whispered as she carefully lifted the gown from the closet.

"It is beautiful, and you look exquisite in it. You do know it's granny's dress, right?"

Sarah smiled sadly, before she turned back to Cindy, "I can't believe you let me wear it, mom?"

"Well, I just figured with the connection to The Passage of Time, and all you and grandma have been through, you should have her dress. The adjustments were so minor, and it turned out beautifully ..."

"Thank you, mommy. Where do I live?"

"You live right here, my darling, and tonight, you'll move into the home that Daniel and Benjamin had built for you. Your little blue house that overlooks your beautiful horses. Daniel planted daffodils around the porch so that they are in full bloom when you move in, and Benjamin made you a beautiful swing for your porch as your wedding present."

Sarah hooked the gown back onto the closet and sat down beside her mother. "He built me my love story?" She could hardly forget the artist that painted her love story, and she couldn't help but wonder if he knew all about Adelaine Alandrali. "All this, mom, all of it, it's that book, The Passage of Time. Because of that book, I have Daniel. It's special. Those pages are full of magic."

"I know, baby, we'll make sure that it never leaves the bookstore again, and who knows? Maybe someone else will find the magic between those pages someday, who knows? Maybe it will save someone else?"

"I hope so, mommy …" Sarah sprang to her feet when she suddenly realized she had turned thirty years old earlier in the year. "Oh no!"

"What's the matter, Sè?"

"I am old!"

Cindy giggled softly before she strolled over to Sarah, who was standing with her back to a full-length mirror. She took Sarah by her hand, and turned her around, until she was introduced to the reflection, staring back at her.

"Look at you, you are beautiful …"

Reluctantly, Sarah fixated a gaze on the reflection in the

mirror, and after scrutinizing the image staring back at her, she smiled proudly at her echo. She conceded to the fact that she had lost weight, her hair was longer, and a couple of fine lines to many had showed up around her eyes and her mouth.

When she smiled, she surrendered to the veracity that each line on her face had a unique story to tell the world, one she would selectively tell, but one she would cherish, preserve and defend for the remainder of her life.

Her lines each had a story to tell, and each could tell thousands of tales of heartbreak, love, joy, but most of all, of one more last chance. They could tell stories of battles and warfare, of becoming a warrior and of conquering battles the world would not quite understand.

The frown lines between her eyes could bear witness to a love she had once lost, but had found again through a bitter, heart-gutting and torturous battle with a passageway in time.

The same lines that would remind her of her heartache after losing Daniel Kingsley, of leaving their home town, and then it would remind her of how she fought against time to save him and alter the course her life once took. "I am older, mom, but I wouldn't change a thing. It was all worth it, and if Daniel would ask me to do it again, I would."

She turned around to face her mother, before she took her hands into hers, "I would do it all again, because, I just, I just love him so much. I couldn't live without him then, and I won't be able to now ..."

Cindy squeezed her hands and smiled dismally at her daughter. Before she could respond, there was a faint knock on the bedroom door, "Sarah?"

Her heart almost jolted from her chest when she heard Daniel's voice whisper from the other side of the walls. Sarah smiled when she heard his familiar voice, and hurriedly made her way over to her door.

She could barely wait a moment longer to open the door and fling her arms around him. When she saw him standing there, she was sure her heart would leap right out of her chest,

"Danny ..." She placed her arms protectively around him and buried her head in his chest as she held tightly onto him.

"I'll see you later, my darling ..." Cindy squeezed Sarah's shoulder before she turned to Daniel, "The wedding is in three hours, don't keep her too long!"

Alice VL

Daniel nodded bashfully, holding Sarah conservatively in his arms. Her eyes trailed up at his older, yet more appealing features, and she smiled when she gazed into his frosty eyes. She had hardly noticed that he was carrying a large, wrapped board underneath his arm, and for a moment, she wondered what it was.

"Come sit with me for a while ..." He took her hand and led her to an empty sofa in the corner of her bedroom. When he sat down beside her, he handed her the large, meticulously wrapped board. "After all that happened in our moment in time, I wanted to get you something to remember that time. I wanted you to have something to remember that you fought so bravely and courageously for us. And then, I remembered that you once told me about this ..." He pointed to the board on her lap, before he took in a deep breath, "And, it so happens that I read about it again in your book, A Moment in Time ..." Daniel paused once again as he began unwrapping the oversized, weighty board. "I travelled to the city, and I walked those busy streets for days and days on end, until I found him ..."

Sarah gasped for air when Daniel removed the last of the brown paper, and exposed a painting she had seen and owned once before. Only, it was a painting she had left behind in a whole other lifetime, and could not exist in this one. "Danny, how? How did, how? I don't understand? It's perfect ... it is exactly ..."

She scrutinized the painting while tracing every part of it with her fingertips, as she recognized each element that was painted in, exactly as it was painted in before.

"I told the old man on the corner of that busy street that he once painted the love of my life a love story, and that he added her love on a swing right beside her. There was a sense of recognition in his eyes, and before I could go on, he told me that he remembered her, and that she wanted to hang it above her big, lonely bed like a silvery gown around her. Needless to say, this made no sense to me, but when he handed me the painting, I knew that it was pretty damn close to how you once described it. I also realized that things aren't always going to make sense to me, and that I should have more faith in the unexplained. I shouldn't try to explain things that are way out of my understanding." Daniel paused and frowned slightly when he turned back to Sarah, "He said that he would paint love stories until Adelaine forgave him. He said that he once made the biggest mistake of his life, and that he walks each lifetime in search of her. He said that sometimes those she helps finds him, other times they don't, but he knows that all the moment in times will eventually lead him to her. How sad is that?"

Sarah placed her hand over her mouth, unable to take her eyes off an exact replica of her painting. She knew that she had not once encountered him since she had travelled through the passage of time, and that it was absolutely, and categorically impossible for him to have any memory of an event, that had never taken place. "It's that book, Danny, and the old man, he must be the man who broke her heart? How did he know, if it never happened?"

"I don't know, Sè, but like I said before, not everything will make sense, every single time. I have learned to leave room for things I can't explain, for magic, as you call it. That's enough for me …"

Sarah smiled dejectedly while still unable to take her eyes off Daniel or the painting. "Are you okay, Sarah?"

"I am great, Danny. Everything is perfect."

He grimaced restlessly when he noticed the tears twinkle in her eyes.

"Why are you so sad?"

She smiled again, before she placed her hand on his

cheek.

"I'm not sad, Danny ..." She lowered her hand, before she took in a deep breath. "I know this is going to sound a little strange, actually, a lot strange. I know, but, yesterday, yesterday I was saying goodbye to you at the docks. I don't mean that it feels like yesterday, I mean, yesterday. And today, I wake up and, you're here, and my mother tells me I am marrying you today? It's suddenly March the 22nd, and you're here? I have lost time and missed out on so much. I don't know what we're like? I don't know what we do, or what our dreams are? I don't know if we've made any plans? What have we been doing for the last fourteen years? It makes me sad, because I feel like, like I was absent from my life."

Daniel shook his head, as he tried to make sense of what Sarah was saying.

"I know, Danny, it sounds insane ..."

He squeezed her hand gently, before he smiled admiringly at her, "I believe you, Sè. I have learned to believe you every day for the last fourteen years. What happened then could have been so different. Things could have turned out so badly, but you saved me back then ..."

She smiled wistfully before she wiped a lost tear that had rolled down her cheek.

"Will you marry me, Sarah Swanson? I know you probably have such an enormous gap between then and now, but I would love to spend the rest of my life, telling you the story of our last fourteen years …"

Sarah climbed onto his lap, and placed her arms around his neck, "I would love to marry you today, Daniel Kingsley. I would love to begin the rest of our lives, today, with you. Here. In this lifetime, and now."

He bent down, and picked up her book, "This was almost a horror of a story …"

Sarah took the book from him, and held it against her chest, "It was once. But, Danny, I got one more last chance, and so did you."

"We sure did. Now throw on that wedding gown and meet me at the altar!" Daniel picked her up and turned her around and around. Sarah burst out laughing before she kissed him fervently.

When he placed her down and back on her feet, Daniel cautiously

THE BOOKSTORE SERIES
Passage of Time – Book 1

made his way over to her bedroom door. Before he walked out, he turned around and smiled, "I love you, Sarah, always."

When he closed the door behind him, Sarah felt again for the first time as though the butterflies and bubbles had come back home, into the very core of her. She knew without a doubt, that she was indebted to the fallen angel that remained trapped in the pages of The Passage of Time, for her very own moment in time.

"Through time, through alternate realities, I will love you, through them all." She whispered as she held her wedding dress against her.

Alice VL

Come along with Daniel and I, as we navigate through the rest of our lives, meeting others Adelaine takes pity on. This is all so new to us, but we believe in the magic of those pages, and we know that there will be others who will need us, the same way I needed my mother through my very own moment in time.

THE END

Alice VL

www.ingramcontent.com/pod-product-compliance
Lightning Source LLC
Chambersburg PA
CBHW031359250626
47155CB00004B/1332